THE DRAGON
IN THE
GHETTO
CAPER

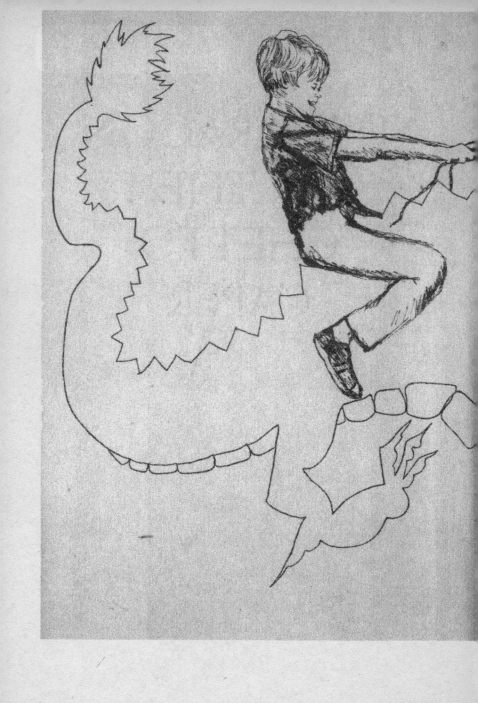

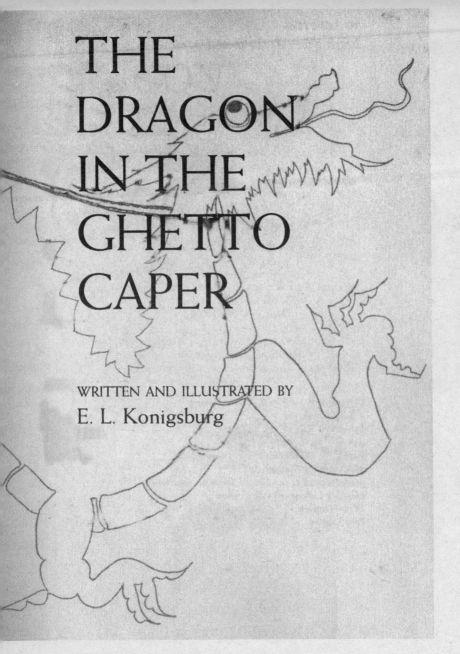

THE DRAGON IN THE GHETTO CAPER

WRITTEN AND ILLUSTRATED BY

E. L. Konigsburg

ALADDIN PAPERBACKS

TO COLETTE—
because we ride the same dragon

Aladdin Paperbacks edition November 1998

Aladdin Paperbacks
An imprint of Simon & Schuster Children's Publishing Division
1230 Avenue of the Americas
New York, NY 10020

The Library of Congress has cataloged the hardcover edition as follows:
Library of Congress Catalog Card Number 74-75563
ISBN 0-689-82328-2 (pbk.)

Other Aladdin Paperbacks
by E. L. Konigsburg

CHAPTER ONE

One of the things that Andrew J. Chronister never did was to attend music class. They could not make him, and they knew it. He could not carry a tune, and he knew it. *They* was the Emerson Country Day School.

Andy had gone to Emerson C.D.S. (Country. Day. School.) for almost seven years, counting kindergarten. The policy there was not to *make* Andrew go to music but to make him *want* to go. They never succeeded. So when the other students went to singing, Andy went to the art room where he drew dragons. Sometimes he painted dragons. One was made out of papier-mâché, and two were made out of construction paper, burlap and Elmer's glue; those took four music lessons each and were the largest.

Dragons, however, were not Andy's true passion; crime was. He was determined to be a detective when he grew up. Not an ordinary police detective. A famous one. Famous, tough and cool. Like Ellery Queen, for God's sake.

Immediately after he had decided that he would be a (famous) (tough) (cool) detective, Andy had put himself into training. He would be ready to solve the crime of the century the minute it occurred in Foxmeadow. Foxmeadow was where Andy lived, and it met the logical requirements of being the scene of a puzzling murder. That is, when a famous, tough, cool detective like Ellery or Sherlock solved a crime, it always involved a closed group of people. Like guests in a hotel. Or movie stars working on a film. Or travelers on an ocean liner. Foxmeadow met that requirement. It certainly was closed.

Foxmeadow was part of the town of Gainesboro. It was a ring of houses built around acres and acres (eighteen holes) of a championship golf course. Plus four tennis courts and one swimming pool, Olympic sized. There were only seven named streets and 126 houses in Foxmeadow. But it was home and the whole world to the people who lived there. A fence circled all around it, and a security guard was posted at the only gate. The guard checked cars to see if they belonged. Cars that belonged had a plate saying FOXMEADOW in the place where the front license plate should be. The guard stopped the cars that didn't belong and made them sign (name, time and destination) in. No one ever walked into Foxmeadow. Hardly anyone walked inside it either, except people with dogs of the variety that needed to or people on the golf course who didn't take a cart.

Famous murders were mostly done for money. Or jealousy. Or revenge. Andy figured that money was usually the one reason behind the other two. And Foxmeadow had plenty of the real thing: money. Everyone who lived in Foxmeadow was something between very comfortable and very rich. Andy's family was in the middle; their maid did not live in.

His family consisted of himself (age eleven-and-a-half); a mother, Mrs. Chronister; a father, Mr. Chronister; and a sister, Mary Jane, age twenty-two, engaged to be married on May 17 and making a very big fuss about it. Andy called her Cleopatra because she acted like one.

Andy kept track of everything that happened in Foxmeadow. That was part of his training. He practiced being cool, and he practiced observing: houses, power mowers, deodorants; water softeners and work schedules and the brand names of the champagne bottles tossed into the garbage. Andy counted, too: French poodles (seventeen), garbage compactors (two, but they were catching on fast), Yamahas and Princess telephones. And wedding gifts; his sister had already received a fondue set and two silver coffeepots (one was inherited). Andy also volunteered. He had collected for the Heart Fund, Cancer Crusade, Mother's March Against Birth Defects, Arthritis, Kidneys, Muscular Dystrophy and Cystic Fibrosis. He figured that if one disease could not get him into someone's house, another disease, another month, would.

Andy would be ready the minute a murder was committed in Foxmeadow. He would put all his clues together, gather all his suspects around him and make brilliant deductions. Besides the actual murder, he lacked only one other thing: a sidekick.

Every cool, tough, famous detective had one: a buddy, a pal, someone who ran his errands, someone who understood his needs and who took care of the details. Someone who did what had to be done—even if it was only asking the right questions. Like Sherlock Holmes had Dr. Watson, and Nero Wolfe had Archie Goodwin, and Charlie Chan had Number One Son. But he didn't have anyone yet.

He had tried the kids in Foxmeadow. They weren't interested in any kind of training unless it involved athletics. They were all jocks. He had tried Theodore Patterson, Jr., and Harley Preston III, two of his classmates who didn't live in Foxmeadow; they weren't interested either. He had gone to their houses, three times each, but they always did it partly wrong. Like they wanted to give orders as well as take them. And that was not the way a real sidekick worked. The only kind of order a sidekick was supposed to give was, "Be careful, sir" or "Be careful, boss." *Boss* or *sir*, it didn't matter to Andrew.

After Theodore and Harley and two jocks from Foxmeadow had failed, Andy had thought of using Timothy Feagin, the daytime security guard at Foxmeadow. An older, crotchety character with a charming brogue might work out. And Timothy was already in the business, so to speak. But Andy soon discovered that being a security guard was just a job to Timothy Feagin. He was more interested in getting home to his TV and his beer than he

4

was in fingerprints or handwriting. Besides, Timothy had a bad habit of tugging at his crotch all the time. Andy didn't know where to look when Tim did that, and he always ended up staring at Tim's crotch, something he found very distracting.

As a detective Andrew was supposed to be slightly hard to get along with, in a lovable sort of way; he figured that he already met that requirement. He was hard to get along with, but lovable. Not like his sister Mary Jane. She was hard to get along with but not in any lovable sort of way. He was supposed to be very observant, very cool and was supposed to like the nice things that money can buy without caring very much about money itself. There was another kind of detective, the rough-'em-up, sweaty kind. That was not what he would be. He saw himself as meeting all the requirements of being the kind of detective he wanted to be except that he needed a sidekick. Only rough-'em-up, sweaty detectives like those on television did without.

He was at a low point in his search for a sidekick when he met Mrs. Harry Yakots, named Edith or Edie. She was hardly what Andy had in mind; she was twenty-nine years old and married, for God's sake.

Andy met her after school on the day that she had gone to the meeting of the Foxmeadow Garden Circle. It was the first meeting of the new year and the first one that Edie had ever attended. Edie liked to grow things. She had planted the seed from every avocado she had ever eaten, and she had been talking to plants for a long time before anyone told her that it was good for them. Edie's plants would start growing every which-a-way before growing straight up (or down). Edie herself would start talking every which-a-way before talking straight up. (She never talked down to anyone.)

Edie went to the Garden Circle meeting thinking that it would give her a chance to talk to someone besides plants. She also wanted to learn about growing day lilies and kumquats. But the ladies didn't know anything about kumquats except what they looked like (shining orange cocoons). And they talked to each other more than Edie. After the meeting was called to order, they talked about their project, which had something to do with gardening, one degree removed. The ladies raised money for the men at the prison farm in Chawtahawnee. The men at the prison farm in Chawtahawnee gardened; they grew vegetables and camellias and leatherleaf fern, and one club member reported that they were growing marijuana between the rows of tomatoes. The president of the Garden Circle made a motion, and the treasurer seconded it, that they form a committee to investigate the marijuana rumors, but they couldn't find a committee. No one in the Garden Circle could tell a tomato plant from a marijuana. Edie could, but she didn't think she should admit it at the first meeting she had ever attended.

The program for that meeting was to visit the art exhibit at Emerson C.D.S. where most of the ladies had a child going to or graduated from. Emerson actually sat on the edge of Foxmeadow; part of the Foxmeadow fence surrounded it, but no one walked there from the meeting. The school was five fairways distant. All the ladies offered each other rides. Edie would have liked to walk, but she accepted a ride from two of the ladies. She rode in the back seat alone, and the ride didn't take long enough for them to become intimate or even well acquainted.

As the ladies walked from one picture to another and talked about detergents and creativity, Edie visited each picture. She smiled at some and tilted her head, puzzled, at others. But when she came to Andy's dragon, she stopped looking. She knew what she wanted to do, and she did it.

She went to the office of the headmaster and asked if she could please purchase the dragon that was on the left wall as you entered the media center. (The media center used to be called the library before it got married to a slide projector and two tape recorders.) The secretary in the Office of the Headmaster said that she would tell Andrew J. Chronister that there was a customer for his dragon.

"How do you know that it is his?" Edie asked.

"Because," the secretary answered, "if it's a dragon, it must be Andy's. This is the fourth year I've been at Emerson, and I can't remember him drawing or painting anything that isn't a dragon. Even when the assignment was to do a self-portrait, his came out a dragon. That was in the third grade."

"I often feel dragonish," Edie said. "He probably felt it that day. I think that it's perfectly all right to do a dragon as a self-portrait, personally."

"Oh," the secretary replied, "I'm sure it was all right, considering that when he was asked to do a family portrait, his mother, father and sister all turned out to be dragons, too. That was fourth grade. You might say that Andrew J. Chronister is a dragon master."

Edie smiled. "Like George and Michael."

"George and Michael who?" the secretary asked.

"Saints," Edie said. The secretary still looked puzzled. "Saint George and Saint Michael. They mastered dragons."

The secretary said, "Yes . . . well . . ." and then asked for Edie's name, address and telephone number and told her that she would give Andrew the message. And she did.

CHAPTER TWO

Andy was the first one off the bus when it stopped
at the gate to Foxmeadow. He was always the first
one off so that he could walk straight ahead. If he
wanted company, he would lag behind until someone
caught up. He didn't usually lag. There wasn't much he
wanted to say to the jocks who lived in his neighborhood.
Even the girls of Foxmeadow were jocks; they stayed
jocks until the seventh grade when they became
Cleopatras like Mary Jane. He waved at Tim to show him
that he wasn't ignoring him; Tim waved back and yelled,
"Hi, Andy," and gave a good yank you-know-where; Andy
watched, hypnotized, but certain that he had made the
right decision in not asking Tim to be his sidekick.

He pulled the note from between pages 112 and 113
of his math book. He had been in math class, problem 14
on page 112, when the secretary had given it to him. He
decided that he would visit Mrs. Yakots rather than telephone her. He had not been inside that house since the
Yakotses had moved in. Everyone said that the Yakotses
were just renting from the Grants who had lived there

before, but no one who said it had taken time to ask and find out.

"Good afternoon," Andy said using his Heart and Cancer voice (those were his favorites). "I am Andrew J. Chronister. How are you today?"

"Yes, I am," Mrs. Yakots said, her glasses catching the late afternoon sun. "Won't you please come in and talk about buying and selling. The dragon."

Andrew accepted her invitation. He walked into the foyer and looked around slowly and carefully as he had trained himself to do.

Mrs. Yakots watched Andy's slow ceiling-to-floor, wall-to-wall gaze. She panicked. "What's the matter? What's the matter?"

"Nothing's the matter," Andy answered. "I like your house a lot." And Andy did. He was surprised that he did. Nothing matched, but, somehow, everything went together.

Mrs. Yakots sighed with relief. "We thank you very much," she said. "My husband is out of town. That's where I want to hang him. His name is Harry," she said, pointing to a spot over the sofa. "How much would it take?"

She had a strange way of talking, Andy observed. But he understood her, he further observed. "I haven't set a price," he said. "Yet," he added. "But I will in a minute." He looked around and decided that things did not match because she didn't want them to, not because she couldn't afford for them to. "Twelve fifty," he said, figuring that he'd have to come down to ten. "And it's a girl."

"It was real friendly of you to stop by—have you ever sold a girl dragon before—instead of phoning."

"Not a boy either," Andy answered. He was pleased with his perfect understanding of her. "I've never even had one framed. My mother doesn't care for my subject matter. I do dragons; she likes flowers. Listen, I could let you have it for ten."

"Oh, I do, too," Mrs. Yakots replied. "That's why I went to that meeting of the Garden Circle. I thought they grew flowers and grass. Lawn grass. Would you take an even seven fifty?"

"Seven fifty isn't even, but it will be okay," Andy replied. "But only because I'm not going to be a famous artist when I grow up. You realize that you can't count on your investment growing. I am going to be a detective when I grow up. A famous one."

Mrs. Yakots then asked Andy if he would like a Coke. Andy said yes and followed her into the kitchen. He wanted to see it; kitchens were another thing he watched. He looked this one over slowly and carefully and asked, "What color do you call this, for God's sake?"

"Mauve," Mrs. Yakots answered. "Harry—he's my husband—and I painted it. I couldn't make the painter understand."

Andy looked up at the ceiling, all swirled with mauve and violet and said, "I can understand that. I can certainly understand that." He sat on a bench across the kitchen table from Mrs. Yakots. The bench was painted a brilliant pink. He rested his hand on its arm and said, "I'm surprised that I don't get burned. I've heard of hot pink, but this is positively electrifying."

Mrs. Yakots smiled. "I painted it myself. I couldn't make the painter understand that either. That's a pew."

"Oh, I wouldn't say that," Andy replied.

"But it is. A church pew. It's from an old church that had Sister Henderson. They were remodeling the church, and she was in charge of selling. That's how I began carrying her every Thursday."

"You carry your sister every Thursday?"

"She's not my sister. Everyone at the Mt. Zion Baptist Church is a Sister, except the men; they're Brothers. She's a church sister in the car. I started taking her the day I bought the bench from her church. They were Black. Both the congregation and the bench. Now just the congregation is. See, I've painted the pew. Pink goes nicely in a mauve kitchen, don't you think?"

Andy was resting his elbow on the table, leaning his head on his fist, sorting out what she had said, "Oh, yeah," he said. "Pink pews would hardly go in a Black church."

Mrs. Yakots rested her elbow on the table and leaned her fist in a pose just like Andy's. "So you want to be a detective?" she asked, eyes blinking at him behind her glasses.

"Yeah," Andy replied, "I've put myself in training. I'm very observing." He closed his eyes and said, "You are five feet six inches tall, weigh 120 and are 36-25-35 . . ." He opened his eyes and looked at Mrs. Yakots, waiting for her to express amazement.

She did. "Gee, Andrew, that's great."

"Not so great," Andy replied. Then afraid that her understanding might be as mixed-up as her talking, he added, "Look, I don't mean that your 36-25-35 isn't great. That is great. I mean my knowing isn't so great. I told you I'm trained. Besides, I saw you swimming two weeks ago. You're nice looking without your clothes or your glasses. I watch swimmers. You swim the way you talk. Uncoordinated." Mrs. Yakots, who had been smiling, suddenly was not; she lowered her head. "Listen," Andy said, hating himself for feeling as bad as he did about making her feel bad. "Listen, five dollars will be perfectly all right for the dragon. Five dollars will certainly be plenty. Plentiful."

"I'll pay on delivery," Mrs. Yakots said. "Harry—he's my husband—thought I needed to get out of the house. That's why I tried swimming. It's worth seven fifty, that's for sure, but I'll take it for five. And I went also to the Garden Circle. But it was worth it to meet someone in Foxmeadow who likes dragons. That's why I take Sister Henderson on her errands every Thursday. Harry travels all week. That means he's only home on the weekends. You know the weekend: Saturdays and Sundays. We are mostly married on the weekends."

"What are you the rest of the week?"

"Edie," she answered. "Edie and alone."

"Listen," Andy said, "I just remembered. The art show is over tomorrow. I'll bring you my painting after school tomorrow. Will you be here?"

14

"If you say so," Mrs. Yakots answered.

Andy said good-bye and walked home. There were a lot of things that he had to sort out. Mrs. Yakots talked a smorgasbord. He had to choose one or two things he could digest. Pink pews and Sister Henderson. Dragons and Thursdays. Edie and alone. Edie and alone. It hadn't occurred to him that there could be an Edie and alone. A pretty, nearsighted thing like her. A grown-up pretty person like her, for God's sake.

Chapter Three

Andy had told Mrs. Yakots that the art show would be over, so the next day he took his dragon down from the left wall of the media center. The other pictures could stay there the rest of the week, but the show would be over for him. In place of his picture he hung a card that he had prepared at home.

Gone elsewhere for the rest of the (exhibit) time. by, Andrew J. Chr.

He carried his painting on the bus, up the street and to the door. He didn't even have to ring. She opened the door and said, "Call me Edie," first thing. Then she took the painting from Andy and looked at it and said, "It is beautiful, Andrew."

Andy was more pleased than a cool, tough person ought to be. "It's a girl, remember," he said. Then he added, "You may call me Andy. A lot of people do."

Edie carried the dragon to the sofa and propped it against the wall, using the back of the sofa as a ledge. "She's beautiful, Andy. Harry—he's my husband—was married before, but I never was, so I've never bought a dragon or any painting before. But he has. With his first wife, but she never bought a dragon. She didn't like or even understand them." She turned from the dragon to Andy and asked, "Will you help me pick out a frame?"

"I believe that I can find the time," Andy replied. "Would tomorrow be too late?" Edie was looking at the (girl) dragon and smiling, showing all of her teeth. Andy cleared his throat. "As a matter of fact, I'm free tomorrow afternoon. We have half-day on Thursdays at Emerson. I could get a note from home to be excused from riding the bus."

"I wrote you a check already," Edie said. "I don't know if your parents would want you to get involved with carrying Sister Henderson. I always finish with Sister by three, and then we could get her framed. For five dollars," she said, handing the check to Andy.

"You happen to have a pretty handwriting," Andy said.

"I'm noticing handwritings. I notice everything I can. It's not easy training to be a detective in Foxmeadow. I can't find a sidekick among all the jocks who live here, and I haven't seen even one murder yet. I begged my father to move into a high crime area, but he refused. He says I've got to be protected because he and Mom don't have much time."

"Oh, I'm so sorry," Edie said. "What is it? Cancer? Heart condition?"

"No. Nothing like that. Golf, a busy law practice for my dad. With my mother, it's tennis and clubs and my sister's wedding. With my sister, it's her wedding and her parties. She spends a lot of time in front of the mirror. She also shops a lot."

"Harry—he's my husband—and I didn't have any parties. We just got married to each other. His daughter was there and her two children. She has one of each: a boy and a girl. Harry—he's my husband—is gone all week, and he wanted me safe, too. That's why I'm protected here, too. Sometimes here you have to go out to find a dragon. That's why I was so surprised at the Garden Circle to find one on the wall at Emerson. Do you want to help me carry Sister Henderson in the car? She lives in the northern part of town."

"Is that where the ghetto is?"

"One of them," Edie said.

Andy said that he wouldn't mind going. He told Edie to pick him up at Emerson C.D.S.

Andy raced home and wrote a note, excusing himself

from riding the bus. He wanted to go so badly that he wasn't going to take *no* for an answer, so he decided not to ask. Since he had started his training, he had stopped asking his parents to sign his report cards. He always did his own. He was something of an artist at it. He decided to write the note in his father's handwriting, which he figured he did seven and one-half percent better than his mother's. It was more man to man.

Mrs. Yakots was waiting for Andy the next day when school let out. But she was not waiting with the other ladies who were picking up children. The others were neatly lined up in the driveway; one by one they pulled up to the curb by the front door of Emerson. Their car doors opened, sometimes from within and sometimes from without, and one by one, the cars filled with kids, kindergarten through six, and then pulled away from the curb making room for the next in line. Mrs. Yakots didn't do that. She had arrived twenty minutes early and had parked. She had gotten out of the car and stood waiting by the side of the building while her car stood blocking the end of the driveway.

Andy came blinking out of the building and looked down the line of cars and saw the empty, parked one. He noticed all the other cars swinging around it, the drivers making faces and muttering. His heart sank. He knew whose car was creating the bottleneck. He knew. He started walking toward it when he felt a tap on his shoulder and heard Edie say, "Hi, there. Here am I, your sidekick, right behind your back."

Andy knew that every student, K through six, and every driver of every car had heard. "You're not my sidekick, for God's sake," he snarled, walking rapidly toward the car.

"Well, you said that you were having trouble with the jocks, and I'm no jock. You know that. You saw me swim."

"We'll discuss it later," Andy said. "But not here." Andy walked as fast as he could through the postschool crowd, wishing that night would suddenly fall. He got to the car a few strides ahead of her, opened the back door, jumped in, slouched down, all the way to the floor and said, "Okay, Yakots, let's move it, and don't spare the treads."

Edie stepped on the gas and pulled away with a screech of rubber. Every teacher, K through six, looked up. Two of them took down the color and make of the car, and one made a note of the license plate number.

"What's the matter, Andy?" Andy didn't answer. He had about 200 degrees to go through before he was cool. "What's the matter, Andy?" she repeated.

Andy poked his head over the rim of the front seat and answered, "Nothing. Nothing is the matter. I do this. It's part of my training. I don't look where I'm going or whether we're turning right or left. That way, when I'm a famous detective, and murderers blindfold me, I'll be able to know how far they've taken me and in which direction."

"Gee, Andy, that's real smart. And I'm happy that by the time you become a famous detective, murderers won't be knocking famous detectives unconscious on the head anymore, the way they do now."

"Well," Andy said, "well," he repeated. "Well, I don't intend to become unconscious. I'm going to train myself to be conscious at all times."

"Sometimes they're stuffed into a trunk, which is very hard to breathe in. It's probably not the real detective though. It's probably a dummy in the movies," Edie added.

Andy said nothing more. He climbed into the front seat and fastened his seat belt. He decided that if this was his big chance to see the ghetto, he ought to see the ghetto. Besides they were well away from Emerson now. No one would see him riding with a crazy lady, and he could observe.

The ghetto was streets with sidewalks and no trees. Foxmeadow was the opposite: trees and no sidewalks. The ghetto had the following: front porches with people sitting on them, a big hospital and clinic named St. Vincent's and laundry hanging out to dry on clotheslines in backyards or strung between houses. (Andy had never seen a clothespin until he was in the fourth grade. The art teacher had given one to each member of his class to make a Christmas tree decoration. Andy had made a dragon out of his.)

The houses on Sister Henderson's street looked like dull aluminum foil except for the potted plants that lined some of the porches. Some old ladies on the front porches were darning. Andy had to ask Edie what they were doing, and she told him. That was the first he learned that *darn* was something besides being a substitute for *damn*. Edie knew a lot about the ghetto. She told Andy that she had been carrying Sister Henderson for four weeks already. This was her fifth.

Sister Henderson was waiting on her porch when they arrived. She wore a hat and carried a large pocketbook and a brown paper bag. She climbed into the back seat of the car showing a rainbow display of girdle and garters, and sat with her purse and her package on her lap and her dignity all around her.

Edie introduced them. Andy and Sister Henderson exchanged hellos, and then Sister Henderson told Edie that they ought to start with Sister Coolidge again today. They went up one ghetto street and down another until they came to Sister Coolidge's house. Edie noticed that there were people out on the streets, some walking, others just loafing. He never remembered seeing anyone standing on the streets of Foxmeadow.

When they arrived at Sister Coolidge's house, Sister Henderson got out of the back seat with her pocketbook, her bag and her dignity and returned with her pocketbook, two bags and her dignity. She was not gone long. They made six more stops, and Sister Henderson ended up with an assortment of bags, brown paper to plastic from Lester's, the shoe store.

The last stop was at Brother Banks's. He lived beyond the bus line; the road leading to his house was not paved; it was two sandy ruts, the size and width of car tires, with a hump of patchy grass between them. Huge bushes of oleanders lined both sides of it. They had to pull off to one side to make way for a car coming in the opposite direction. Sister Henderson waved to the driver of the other car. "Brother Maytag be early this week," she said.

Brother Banks's house sat alone, squatting on its concrete block supports, like a giant grand piano on sawed-off legs. Sister Henderson stayed at Brother Banks's longer than she did at the other stops.

"What church are these donations for?" Andy asked.

"Sister Henderson's, I guess."

"Is Brother Banks their minister?"

"Brother Banks is their Minister of Finance, I guess."

After they had finished and as Sister Henderson was disembarking in front of her own house, Andy turned to her and said, "It was very nice meeting you." He spoke very loud and very slow. "Nice ghetto you've got here."

"It's home t' me," Sister Henderson replied. "'Bye, y'all come back now, y'heah?"

"Uh, Andy," Edie said after they were at the second red light past Sister's house, "most people live in a house on a street."

"So?"

"So that's the way they think of themselves. Like Sister Henderson. She'd say that she lives on Rutgers. Like she would say that she lives on Rutgers Avenue. Like she'd say that she lives at 9819. Like she doesn't think of her home as being in a ghetto."

"How can someone live in a ghetto and not think it? Look at the houses. They don't have any paint, for God's sake."

"Well, they *know* it, the way you know that you live in Foxmeadow. But they don't expect to be told they live in a ghetto any more than you do."

"Any more than *I* do?" Andy replied. "Well, I see nothing wrong with calling a spade a spade or calling a ghetto a ghetto."

There followed a vacuum in the car. Edie said nothing, and Andy did not interrupt her. Finally, Andy broke the silence. As they passed a Carvel, he asked Edie if she would like a frozen custard. "I'll treat," he said.

Edie allowed him to. They smiled at each other over twin peaks of vanilla covered with chocolate sprinkles. Then they drove to Century Arts and Crafts where they spent an hour and ten minutes selecting a frame. The man behind the counter, who saw at least sixty-five paintings a week (about three per week were uglies painted on velvet), admired Andy's dragon before he said, "That'll be twenty-six fifty-two with tax. Ready next Thursday morning. We open at nine."

"We can't be here until after three," Andy said.

"Yes," Edie agreed, "we have Sister stops before we ever get here."

And that was the cool way that Andy announced that he wanted to accompany Edie next week, and that was the sweet way she accepted.

CHAPTER FOUR

Andy stopped at Edie's every day after school except on Thursdays when she picked him up from Emerson. And except on Fridays when the weekend began, and she was mostly married. Andy spent as much time with Edie Yakots as he did with his family. It was the most concentrated friendship he had ever had. But she wasn't a friend; she was his secret sidekick.

Andy found that going places and doing things with Edie was fine as long as they were alone. It was even fun. But it was altogether embarrassing to go or to do with her in front of anyone else in Foxmeadow or in front of anyone from Emerson. She always did some part of it wrong. For example, he had trained her to drive around to the front of the school and to wait with the other cars on Thursday; she did that part just like a normal woman. But when she saw Andy, she waved like an antenna in a high wind. A cool, tough person doesn't appreciate that. But Edie said that she was always so glad to see Andy that her enthusiasm overcame her training. And any cool, tough person has to be glad to hear that. Even if that cool, tough person doesn't care to show that he is glad.

Edie never cared if her enthusiasm showed. Hers wasn't like the enthusiasm of the jocks of Foxmeadow. They screamed and cheered at football games and swimming meets, and their excitement was over when the action was. Edie could be enthusiastic about slow motion as well as fast. There isn't much slower motion than plants growing in a garden, and Edie got excited about that. The subtropical climate of Gainesboro allowed two gardens a year, and she had started a winter garden the week they had met.

On his first few visits Andy had not done any work in the garden. He would only watch and hand-to-her and get-for-her, but he soon found that he had an opinion about where the dwarf azaleas should go. Since he never held an opinion for longer than two minutes before expressing it, Andy told Edie where he thought the dwarf azaleas should go. She listened; she agreed; and Andy was soon helping her dig and fertilize, which was more suitable. Fetching and carrying was work for a sidekick.

After their work was done, Edie would fix them both Cokes (she always used crushed ice and added a maraschino cherry and a swizzle stick) and tell Andy about her life before she had moved into Foxmeadow. Either her talking smoothed out or else Andy got professional at unscrambling her sentences; she became more interesting than confusing.

She had had a lot of jobs. Not the ordinary Foxmeadow jobs like plastic surgeon or tax consultant or

27

corporation president. Edie had had interesting jobs, and she had been fired from them. Not like the people of Foxmeadow who simply got promoted out of one job and into another. Edie had actually been fired.

She had first chosen jobs where she wouldn't have to make conversation. Once she became a vacuum cleaner demonstrator at a home show. While a salesman talked about how wonderful the vacuum cleaner was, Edie was supposed to smile and sweep. She thought she would look more glamorous without her eyeglasses, so she didn't wear them. She accidentally sucked the hem of her skirt into the vacuum and burned out the motor. She got fired for nearsightedness and indecent exposure.

She decided that if she had to do some talking, she could do it if she had a prepared speech. So next she got a job making telephone calls for a real estate developer. She soon started getting obscene answers. When she called the telephone company to complain, they told her that they hardly knew what to do about obscene phone calls, but they had a very simple solution to obscene phone answers: don't make the calls. When she told her boss, he agreed with the telephone company, and he fired her.

Edie moved from one job to another until she got brave enough to become an airline stewardess. In that line of work she smiled more than she spoke, and she always immediately did what was asked so that she would have less to explain. She was getting good at saying things like "welcome aboard" and "please fasten your seat belts" when she spilled a whole stainless steel container of salad dressing (creamy Roquefort) over an important executive of the airlines. But he didn't fire her. He married her. He was Harry Yakots.

Sometimes Edie would make Andy laugh out loud. He figured that it was all right to allow that. A sidekick usually was an amusing fellow. Even though this amusing fellow was an amusing girl.

Sometimes on his way home from her house Andy would wonder why Edie took so much time to tell him things about herself. Of course sidekicks often were talkative. He also reasoned that she talked a lot because they had more to catch up on with each other. The other kids, the jocks at Emerson, knew all about each other already. There was nothing to tell. They never held jobs. They were all so much alike that they could have interchangeable parts. Edie was different, bordering on strange, and it was perfectly all right for her to think she was his sidekick as long as they kept quiet.

Valentine's Day came on Tuesday, but Andy had finished his during Monday's music lesson. He looked at what he had done and decided that his mother had a perfect right to think that dragons were inappropriate on valentines. On the other hand, he had a perfect right to think that they were not. He also decided that he would use some of his money to buy his mother a Hallmark. This year he would give his dragon valentine to Edie Yakots. He pressed his work between the pages of his social studies book. Besides being the only valentine at Emerson C.D.S. that had a dragon, his was the only one that had no cupids.

Edie was in the yard when Andy walked up. "Hi, Andrew J. Chronister," she yelled. "I'm spreading cow-do on my snapdragons."

"Let's go inside," Andy said.

Edie wiped her hands on the back seat of her jeans. She held the door open for him, and as he walked through ahead of her, she said, "Some people shorten their name."

"You mean that Yakots was even worse before it was shortened?"

"I was talking about my snapdragons, the flowers I was putting the cow-do on," Edie said, washing her hands at the kitchen sink. "Some people call them snaps. But I don't. I call them by their whole rightful name, snapdragons. Because I like the dragon part the best."

"Oh, for God's sake, Yakots, I've never heard a grown lady call it that before."

"Well, don't be surprised. You know how I believe in dragons."

"I don't mean the snapdragons, for God's sake. I mean the cow manure. I've never heard a grown woman call it *cow-do* before."

"But you knew what I meant."

"Of course I knew what you meant."

"Well? See? Harry—he's my husband—says that speech is communication."

Andy decided to change the subject. "Did you have a nice marriage this weekend?"

"Very nice, thank you. Did you have a nice detecting?"

Edie had poured them both Cokes. Andy carried his into the den, sat down, leaned back, swung his arm over the back of the sofa and crossed his legs. "Oh," he sighed. "I thought of getting into something new this weekend— memory."

"Memories are old, not new," Edie said. "If they're not in the past, they're a *now*, not a memory."

"Oh, Yakots, can't I make you understand? I'm working on improving my memory." Andy told her about a famous author who had done a study of two murderers. Instead of using tape recorders while he was doing the interviews, he had used his memory. He had practiced so that he could repeat whole conversations. That way the murderers weren't self-conscious about talking into a microphone. Andy had decided that this kind of training would be as extremely useful for a famous detective as it was for a famous author.

Edie listened with great interest. "I'll help," she said.

"Don't be ridiculous. How can you help? Half the time you talk as if you were born without conjunctions."

"I talk perfectly all right after people know me. Harry—he's my husband—says that I taper toward normal. I think it's nice that he says that I *taper* toward normal. Means that normal is less than what I usually am."

But to strangers, Edie always talked in confetti. And it was that very thing that he had to avoid. It was all right

31

having her as a secret sidekick, but he didn't want to encourage her. When he was famous, she'd have to appear in public, and the public, God knows, is full of strangers.

"Thanks a lot," Andy said, "but I can do without you. I have a cassette player. I'll just read something into it, listen and repeat it into the cassette. Then I'll play that back and listen again."

"Memorizing *reading* isn't the same as memorizing *listening*. Memorizing listening is harder. I'll tell you what. I'll do the reading. You do the listening and memorizing, and I'll check you. It will be faster and more like conversation for you."

Andy thought that no one, but no one, had ever heard of a sidekick helping a detective get trained. Sidekicks took orders and anticipated needs. Allowing someone to help him would make them too equal; you can't get too equal with a sidekick. Imagine Ellery or Sherlock doing that. "I should hope that your helping would be nothing at all like having a conversation with you. Having a conversation with you is like watching a TV program that is out of sync."

Edie looked down at her lap and said very quietly, "I thought you were beginning to understand dragons." She shoved her glasses up on her nose and looked at Andy through their sides.

Dragons made him remember his valentine. He took it out. "By the way, this is for you. It's not due until tomorrow, but I was finished, so I brought it over." He handed it to her.

Let me set your heart on fire, valentine.

by, Andrew J. Chr.

Edie looked at it a long time. Her eyes were shining and saying thank you, but she said nothing. Out loud. Her smile said a lot. No one had ever appreciated his dragons that much. His mother preferred hearts and cupids, and Mary Jane had told him that she thought that he was some kind of pervert, never doing anything but dragons. (Mary Jane had said that when he got older he would read Freud and find out how really weird he was.) And here was Edie, not thinking that he was weird at all. He was more flattered than he thought he should be. "Don't steam your glasses over it," he said. He hadn't meant to say that. He should have thought of a better way, a cool way to show his appreciation of her appreciation.

"May I show it to Harry?" Edie asked. "He understands dragons. He claims that he was married to one for twenty-three years." Andy looked puzzled. "Not me." She added, "I'm not a twenty-three-year wife. His first one was. The one he divorced to marry me." Edie stared at the valentine a bit longer. "Is this one a boy or a girl?" she asked.

"I wouldn't give a girl to a girl for Valentine's Day, for God's sake."

"That's right," Edie said. "I should have known."

He didn't like her feeling guilty about not knowing it was a boy. He hadn't decided what it was until she had asked. "That's okay," he said. "You can show it to Harry if you want to."

"Gee thanks," Edie said. "Isn't there anything I can do to help you? I would love to help you."

"Oh, okay," Andy replied. "I'll bring some stuff over tomorrow, and I'll see how you work out."

"I'm going to try to be great at helping you," Edie said.

"Yeah," Andy answered and left. He closed the door behind him, thinking that he'd find some way to get out of working with her on memory training. What if he decided not to train his memory? Why did he ever agree in the first place? Of course, he hadn't agreed in the first place. He did it in the second. Maybe the third. He was beginning to talk like her, for God's sake. To himself.

CHAPTER FIVE

Shortly after he got home Andy decided to develop laryngitis. That would make him just sick enough to be excused from going to Edie's tomorrow and just sick enough not to participate in the Valentine's Day party at school. But not sick enough to miss it. He preferred observing to participating in Emerson C.D.S. parties.

He decided to practice his laryngitis at the supper table. A cool, tough detective ought to be able to keep up that much of a disguise. He also decided that his laryngitis would be a brown-out, not a black-out; he would allow himself to whisper. He wanted to be able to ask someone to pass the salt if he needed it. He knew he would need it. He used a lot of salt.

"And how was your day, dear?" Mrs. Chronister asked her husband. She always asked that. "Just delicious, and how was yours?" he answered. He always answered that. It was their start, and after you've been married as long as they have, you have to start someplace, Andy thought. From that point each of them began a recitation of what had happened during the day.

His mother usually did less during the day and had more to say. "Mary Jane had a kitchen gadget party at the Hemmings' this afternoon."

"Is that Jan and Ira Hemming?"

"Yes, the couple who live next door to the Grants."

"Not the Grants. The Yakotses," Andy whispered.

"What's the matter, Andrew? You sound as if you have laryngitis in a foreign language. What are Yakotses?" Mr. Chronister asked.

Andy opened his mouth, stuck out his tongue and pointed to his throat. "Sore," he whispered.

"Your tongue or your throat?"

Andy pointed to his throat.

"Then hold your tongue and save your throat, dear," Mrs. Chronister said. She turned to her husband and continued. "The Yakotses are the couple who live in the Grants' house. The Hemmings are still sorry that the Grants had to move. They feel as if they've lost their good right hand. The Grants lived to the right of them, remember? That is the right, as you face the house. Of course, everyone says that the new people are only renting. Strange couple. Very strange. He looks old enough to be her father."

"He is," Andy interrupted.

"He is her father, or he is old enough to be?" Mr. Chronister asked.

"Old enough."

"Very strange," Mrs. Chronister continued. "Jan Hemming said that she tried to be friendly with the woman, but she talks as if she had been born without conjunctions or something." Andy was annoyed at hearing his mother use the exact description he had used. Coming from his mother, it sounded insulting. "It seems that you can't have an actual conversation with her," Mrs. Chronister continued. "And her husband! Why, he's hardly ever home. He must have some sort of traveling job," she said, and then smiling at Mr. Chronister, she added, "or another family tucked away somewhere."

"Yes," Andy whispered.

"He has a traveling job, or he has another family?" Mr. Chronister asked.

"Both," Andy whispered.

"Yes, dear," Mrs. Chronister said. "Save your voice for school tomorrow." His mother appeared to be more interested in continuing her conversation than in getting the facts. "Jan said that the woman is quite friendly. Jan went over to introduce herself when they first moved in, and she said that they have done the strangest things to the Grants' house. An old church pew and odd colors painted on the walls."

"In the kitchen," Andy volunteered.

"The odd colors or the church pew?" Mr. Chronister asked.

"Both."

"Save your voice, dear," Mrs. Chronister continued. "Jan said that the Yakots woman went to the January meeting of the Garden Circle. I was sorry that I couldn't go to that one. It happened to fall on the same day that the

Freemans had that champagne brunch for Mary Jane. Anyway, Jan said that the woman seems to be about Mary Jane's age, poor thing. Here she is, saddled with a husband old enough to be her father, and a house that everyone says they're only renting and that she's painted all these strange colors and no one around that she can talk to, that is, if she could talk . . ."

"She can talk," Andy said. "She can talk just fine, only she happens to take more listening to than most people. It's not like listening to you. A person doesn't have to listen to you very hard because you never say much even when you say a lot. Mrs. Yakots happens to be better at making sense than at making sentences."

"Andrew, you will apologize to your mother."

Andy turned to his father, "What for, for God's sake?"

"For the rudeness of your manner and for saying that your mother never says much."

"I apologize," Andy shouted.

"Andrew seems to have lost his laryngitis along with his temper," Mary Jane said. It was the first thing she had said all during the meal, and, of course, being Mary Jane, it was the worst. Mary Jane always managed to say the first worst thing.

Mr. Chronister looked at his son, interested. "You seem to know this Mrs. Yakots quite well."

"She happens to be a person who admires dragons and who is willing to buy one. And she happens to be a person who is willing to take time out to help a future detective with his training."

"Oh," said Mr. Chronister.

"Oh," said Mrs. Chronister.

"Oh," said Ms. Chronister.

"Uh-oh," said Andy. He realized that in the defense of Edie Yakots he had not only destroyed his disguise, but had also destroyed his excuse for not having her help him. He had not only admitted knowing her, he had committed himself to her. In front of his whole family. At the supper table, for God's sake.

When Andy went to his room, he took his catalogs down from his bookshelf. He began to sort them. He wouldn't take them all over to Edie's. He had too many. When he had started his training, he had also begun collecting catalogs and the Thursday editions of the local paper. The Thursday edition ran the grocery ads. Sometimes Andy made charts of the cost of Ivory soap or paper towels, pricing out the cost per sheet, not the cost per roll. He had thought that it would be good analytical training. But he hadn't had time to do that lately, what with helping Edie with the garden and carrying Sister Henderson every Thursday afternoon. The research he did on the grocery ads never mattered to his mother, anyway. She went to one grocery store and 400 dress shops per week and bought whatever she needed. If the grocery store was out of something, she waited until she went back the next week. "Better the stores should run their legs off than I should," she explained. People in Foxmeadow hated walking unless it was for some jock thing like golf or for shopping for no purpose—like dresses.

* * * *

When Edie answered the door the next day, Andy handed her the catalogs. He was curt and businesslike. He explained that he had chosen J.C. Penney because the descriptions were short and full of detail. He particularly recommended the hardware section. It was the way most conversation was: short and detailed like hardware.

"Not in real life," Edie replied. "Sometimes a lot of people don't even talk anymore. Even those people who are perfectly able to do it correctly. And even those people who don't have to use their own words, like actors. Actors hardly talk anymore. Just last weekend, Harry— he's my husband—and I went to a movie that was supposed to be very realistic. It was even rated R, and it was mostly all grunts."

Andy's eyes flew to the ceiling. "Listen, Yakots. I decided that we'll practice details, okay? Let's start."

"If you say so. But I think it's harder to remember loose conversation than tight conversation. Like if I call you up, do you say *hi* or *hello* or what?"

"I never say *what?*"

"And that's a good thing, too. Too many people say *what?* They say it even before they finish listening. Now, for myself, I hardly ever say *what?* Because, being a handicapped talker, I am a good listener. Just the way the blind are good feelers. Being a good listener, I notice that most people talk in sounds more than sentences and that they say *you know* to fill in the spaces."

"That may be so, Yakots, but when I get my suspects

40

together to explain how all my clues led up to my finding the murderer, I'll have to talk in sentences. I'll have to show everyone step by step how I arrived at my conclusion. How my observations of every little detail, every little piece of the puzzle led me to the murderer. Now, Yakots, let's begin."

"But, Andy, what you just said was about *your* talking, not about other people's. You said that you wanted to practice memorizing what you *hear*."

"Listen, Yakots, what you're saying may make sense, but if you're interested in being a sidekick, you'll do it my way."

Edie turned to the hardware section of the catalog, read a little and looked up at Andy. "Surprised?" she asked.

"Surprised, Yakots? At what?"

"At how well I read? I get it all straight just the way it is written down. It's only when I open my mouth to let out my own words that the dragon enters. And only until I really know you."

"Do you want an Academy Award for reading a hardware catalog, or can we continue, Yakots?"

Edie smiled and said, "Sure, boss."

That *sure, boss* didn't come out garbled. As a matter of fact, it came out exactly right. Andy nodded at Edie. Perhaps having her help him wasn't too bad an idea.

CHAPTER SIX

By the last part of that same week, Andy's interest in memory training grew as thin as February's dawn's early light. He walked to Edie's as soon as the school bus dropped him off, and he inspected their garden. Now that it was beginning to whisper color, there was little left to do for it, except water, and that was best done early in the day, long before he got out of school.

Edie gave him a glass of Coke and set out a dish of olives for him. She had discovered that Andy liked green olives better than cookies, so she kept some on hand for him. Then Edie began reading the linen section of the Sears catalog. She had not even mentioned prices when Andy interrupted. "What do you think we'll find in the ghetto this week?"

"A detour. I read in the paper that they're building an addition to St. Vincent's Hospital."

"That's not what I mean, Yakots. I mean what kind of flags and posters do you think we'll find? It's National Black History Week, for God's sake. I thought that everyone knew that. I expect to find posters of W.E.B. DuBois and Martin Luther King and Mary McLeod Bethune."

"I don't think you'll find anything different except the detour because of the hospital."

"But it's *National* Black History Week, and Gainesboro is part of the nation, for God's sake. And Mary McLeod Bethune was president of a college that is practically next door to Gainesboro, for God's sake."

"Don't expect parades either."

"This is the way I look at it, Yakots. If I had a culture, I sure wouldn't be cool about it. I'd sure celebrate."

"You have a culture."

"I mean a ghetto culture, for God's sake."

"You have a ghetto culture."

"How can you say that, Yakots? I've lived in Foxmeadow all my life. Foxmeadow has no culture. Everyone here is *unanimous*."

They found the detour on Rutgers Avenue, on the Foxmeadow side of Sister Henderson's house. A four-block area was fenced off for hard hats. Because of the detour they had to jog in and out of side streets, and they got lost. Andy was pleased. "You know," he said to Edie as they rode up one street and down another, looking for another part of Rutgers Avenue, "you know, I've never been lost before. Before I put myself into training I used to get on my bike and ride and ride around Foxmeadow and try to get lost. But I never could. The best I could do was to confuse the eighteenth hole and the twelfth, but it's all arranged so that you can find your way back."

"You can't get lost in Foxmeadow. All the dragons are locked out."

"What dragons? For God's sake, Yakots, a guy can't have any kind of serious discussion with you. You keep bringing everything back to dragons. What dragons are you talking about now?"

"Only one. The one you're searching for. The one I'm going to help you find."

"Just find your way out of here for now, Yakots."

Edie did. They had not been long lost, not even long enough for Sister Henderson to get uncomfortable.

"Happy National Black History Week," Andy said as soon as Sister had folded herself into the car.

"So it be," Sister said. "Ah don' hol' too much with Black Hist'ry Week. Ah figgers it's like white choc'lit, somethin' that started out black bein' converted inta somethin' white, an' t' me, it always taste a li'l bit waxy. But I thanks you anyways, Andy."

So for National Black History Week they went on their appointed rounds just as they did every other week. Andy thought about Sister after they got home. She was so sure of what she was that she didn't need a week to remind her. That was the first time that he had ever thought about Sister, instead of thinking about himself in relation to her. She probably had thoughts all the time. She probably had more thoughts than she would ever say. Sister was like her ghetto: full of secrets and a secret kind of dignity.

* * * *

In March their garden got loud with pink. On Mondays, Tuesdays and Wednesdays there was little to do except see and smell. There was a lot of time for memory training. A lot, a lot of time. Andy was grateful for Thursdays.

Edie was reading the fishing equipment pages, and Andy was making more mistakes than he ever had. "I think we ought to start another garden, a garden of wild things," Edie suggested.

"Wild things, Yakots? You mean weeds? You want me to cultivate weeds?"

"Even the most important and dignified flowers were once weeds. Even roses. It's hard to transplant a wild thing like a wild flower or a dragon; for them to grow properly, they need a certain amount of neglect."

"There you go again, Yakots, bringing dragons into the conversation when I'm not interested in dragons. I'm interested in detectiving."

"You're interested in dragons all right."

"I am not. I am not. I am not. They're just what come out when I sit down to draw, for God's sake."

"Which came first?" Edie asked. "The dragons or the detectiving?"

"It's not a question of that—of which came first. The dragons just came. I never decided to draw dragons. They just came. They appear on any paper that I happen to be drawing on. I never make a decision about it."

"Tell me when the first dragon came."

"Are you trying to get out of this memory training,

asking all these questions? Are you trying to distract me?"

"Well, yeah," Edie replied.

"I knew you wouldn't work out as a sidekick, Yakots. Don't consider yourself permanent. You may be replaced at any moment."

"Am I fired, boss?"

"I didn't say that. Just don't be too confident. Just consider yourself *pro tem.*"

Edie looked back down at the catalog. "We were learning hand-tied flies when we left off."

"If you insist on my telling you about my first dragon, I'll tell you about my first dragon." Edie said nothing. "Because I happen to remember my first dragon very well." Edie closed the catalog and looked up, smiling. Andy picked up his glass of Coke, crossed his legs, gave the ice in his glass two stirs, one while looking down and one while looking up. Then he began. "I was in the third grade when it happened. We were in singing class, me and the rest of the third grade, and we were singing. The song we were singing was 'Michael, row the boat ashore, hallelujah.' We were lined up in three rows, the whole third grade of us. Row one started the song, and when they got to *ashore*, row two was supposed to start and then row three. We were also supposed to make rowing motions with our hands and sway back and forth. I was in row one, and it's a known fact that if you ain't got rhythm, music is a lot of work. It's not easy to keep track of the words and row and sway at the same time. Well, everyone, even row three, had finished singing, and everyone had stopped

46

rowing and swaying. Everyone but me. I was concentrating so hard that I didn't realize that everyone else was finished, and I sang a solo for about a hundred or maybe a thousand minutes before I realized that I was doing it.

"After music we had art. We were told to draw Michael rowing the boat ashore. To have you draw what they have you sing is what they call *coordinating the arts* at Emerson. That's when I drew my first dragon. Michael was a dragon. So was his boat."

Edie said, "If I could draw, I would draw a lot of dragons, too."

"Well, I don't do a lot of dragons. I do *only* dragons. They're what come out. And I don't go to music class anymore."

"Now will you tell me why you decided to become a detective?"

"You've had enough for today, Yakots. Maybe I'll tell you more some other time."

Andy wasn't sure that he would tell Edie at all. He was boss. He had to keep some things for himself. Even Sister Henderson did that. After all, he wasn't quite twelve years old, and not much had happened to him. It wasn't like being twenty-nine years old, for God's sake. By the time he would be twenty-nine years old, he expected to have hundreds of happenings and about eight or nine famous cases inside himself. Then he could spare telling. Right now there was no point in telling Edie why he had decided to become a famous detective. He wouldn't tell right now. He'd wait a few years until he knew.

CHAPTER SEVEN

By the Thursday before Easter everyone at the Chronisters was completely involved with the wedding except Mr. who was completely involved with work. That week when Sister Henderson climbed into the back seat of the car, Edie turned to her and said, "I want to make a donation myself this week. For Easter."

Sister Henderson raised her eyebrows. "Why, Ah'm supprized at you, Miz Yakots."

"Why?" Edie asked. It's Easter, and I need total involvement. As it says in the Bible about charity in Matthew, Chapter VI, verse three."

"Well, aw right," Sister said, reaching over the front seat and taking the five dollar bill that Edie held out. "Like you and Matthew say: six three. Do you want it boxed?"

"That won't be necessary," Edie answered.

They completed their rounds in silence, except for an occasional clicking of her tongue by Sister Henderson. When they arrived at Brother Banks's, Sister left the car and started down the path. She stopped, shook her head and returned to the car. "Are you sure you want this *total* involvement?"

"Of course she's sure," Andy said. "What do you think she is? An Indian giver?" He stopped short. "Not that I have anything against the Indians any more than I do against you Blacks. Except maybe your manners."

Sister Henderson paid no attention to him. She closed her eyes and clutched her bags to her and said, "Ah jes don' know what t' say."

"Try *thank you*," Andy suggested.

Sister Henderson continued nodding her head. "Ah jes don' know what t' say, Brother Maytag," she said as Brother Maytag and his friend were walking down the steps of Brother Banks's house.

"Don't worry, sistah," he answered. Brother Maytag and his friend drove out, talking to each other and not even waving to Andy and Edie.

Andy turned toward Edie. "That's another thing about the ghetto. They may have sidewalks and dignity, but they sure don't have manners."

"Don't confuse manners and kindness."

"Don't tell me that. My sister Mary Jane writes a four-page thank-you note for two lousy tea towels, for God's sake. And here, you're giving Sister five whole dollars, and she doesn't even say a thank-you."

"Maybe your sister Mary Jane just likes to write thank-you notes. I did. Of course, we didn't get many presents, Harry—he's my husband—and me. But for those we got, I liked to write thank you. Mostly because it is so hard for me to say it."

"Do you like big weddings?" Andy asked.

"I love them."

"Mary Jane's making a bigger celebration than national Black History. As far as I'm concerned, they're a big waste."

"They're not such a waste. They're a form of theater. If you watch them good, and I'm a good watcher for the same reason that I'm a good listener, you can find the people who have dragons. They're the people to seek out."

Andy hardly noticed that she had mentioned dragons again; he was wondering if the Yakotses were on the invitation list. All the invitations had been addressed, ready to be mailed on Monday. He decided that it would be interesting to check when he got home. It would be nice (and also not nice) if they were invited. If they were, they were. And if they were not, they were not. He, Andy, certainly wouldn't do anything to help one way or another. If Edie came, she would probably wave like a windmill all during the ceremony and talk to everyone all out of sync and embarrass him. To death. In front of all the rest of Foxmeadow plus two families' worth of relatives.

Sister Henderson returned to the car, still shaking her head. "Brother say he supprized at you, too. He say that if you hit, you'll break up the ole Banks." She continued mumbling all the way home. Andy paid no attention.

Construction activity, on the hospital, had picked up, and some of the side streets were temporarily blocked by concrete mixers and sand trucks moving across them. They did not get lost again, but they did get slowed down jogging in and out of side streets; it was past five when they pulled into Edie's driveway.

Andy popped out of the car, "See ya, Yakots," he yelled.

"Wait a minute," Edie said. "I made you pysanky."

"Are you being vulgar again?"

"Come see," Edie insisted.

She led Andy through the house to the kitchen where an old wicker basket, a small one, was sitting on the counter top. Inside the basket were the three most beautifully decorated eggs that Andy had ever seen in his life. No green fake straw. Just the eggs.

Stay cool, Andy thought to himself. Stay cool. "They're neat," he said. He cleared his throat and added, "They're very neat. You might even say that they're extremely neat." Edie watched him, eyes bright, nodding. He looked up and caught her eye. "Oh, well, Yakots, these are absolutely the most gorgeous Easter eggs I have ever

seen in my entire life. How in the world do you do them?"

"They're Ukrainian. My grandmother taught me. They're called *pysanky*. Someone has to make them at Easter. The fate of the world depends on it. If no one makes pysanky, the chained monster will break out and devour us all."

"Do you really believe that?"

"It's an old Ukrainian belief. The Ukraine is part of the USSR."

"I didn't realize that they had dragons in communism."

"Dragons are everywhere. Even on the other side of the world in China. You have to hunt for them in Foxmeadow. The dragon is a necessary creature. You've got to know your dragon, but you've also got to keep him under control. That's why I make pysanky every Easter."

"May I take my eggs home? My pysanky?"

"They're for you and your dragon," Edie said.

Andy started out the door, carrying the basket. He turned and said, "Don't taper any more toward normal, please. When your sentences improve, you become very hard to understand."

"You'll understand me better when you understand your dragon."

Andy opened his mouth to say something but said, "Well, Happy Easter," instead. After he closed the door he leaned against the jamb and whispered, "I think she's nuts, for God's sake. *The dragon is a necessary creature*! I just draw them. She really believes in them, for God's sake!"

His house was still empty when he arrived home. He

carried the basket to his room and put it on the highest bookshelf so that it would be safe. The eggs were safe there, but he couldn't see them. He moved them to his desk. He lay across his bed and couldn't see them while lying down, so he tenderly moved them over to the edge where he could. He lay back down on his bed and smiled at his pysanky. He realized that that was not a cool, tough thing to do. But it was perfectly all right to do it. He was alone, and no one was there for him to be cool for.

He wandered around upstairs, into Mary Jane's room. Presents, boxes of new clothes and honeymoon under-wear and travel folders were heaped on the extra twin bed, on her dresser, on the floor. He wandered back into his room to allow the pysanky to catch his eye as he walked past his desk. Then he went into his parents' room and walked around. The pysanky would never fit on his mother's desk. Hers was covered with two big boxes of invitations, standing on edge like files in a drawer. They were all addressed and stamped. Ready to go. Lying on top of the boxes was a list of those who were invited. His mother would check them off as they accepted by return mail. Seven pages of legal-sized lined yellow paper, stapled together. Andy looked for the Y's. *Yakots* was not there. That settled that. No worry about Edie's acting foolish at the wedding.

He walked back into his room to let the basket catch his eye again. It did. He took it from the desk and lifted the eggs, one by one. What a lot of work went into each.

He wouldn't mind if his mother had invited Edie. She

had invited practically everyone else in Foxmeadow. She could have invited the Yakotses—even if they were only renting.

He examined the eggs again. He wished he had a grandmother who could teach him skills of the Ukrainian tribe. Or any tribe. The only tribal skill his mother could pass down was her tennis forehand. He wished he were Ukrainian. Of course, he didn't believe that about the dragon and the fate of the world. He didn't believe in dragons. He believed in being cool and tough and famous. Now, if Edie were cool, he wouldn't mind if his mother had invited her.

He wandered back into his mother's room. There were stacks of extra invitations and there was a stack of small squares of tissue paper. There were envelopes in three sizes, two with stickum and one without. Invitations to weddings were very complicated. Maybe that was the tribal skill that his mother would pass down to him—invitation assemblage.

They couldn't be that hard to assemble, he thought. Just put smaller parts into bigger parts and put a piece of tissue between each part. That's hardly anything at all to learn, for God's sake. Who did his mother think she was?—passing down a silly bit of a skill like that and not inviting Edie besides. After Edie had gone to all that trouble to make him pysanky.

He returned to his room, carrying the assembled invitation. He took his first and second grade report cards from his desk drawer. Before he had learned to write, his mother had signed all of his school reports. *Vivian J. Chronister.* (He got the *J.* in his name from her, from *Jackson,* his mother's maiden name.) He addressed an invitation to Mr. and Mrs. Harry Yakots in his mother's handwriting, then he walked back to his mother's desk and placed the Yakotses between the Wylies and the Yeagers. His forgery was fine. Quite neat. Ball point pens helped. They made handwriting look loopy and undistinguished.

When he finally sat back down at his own desk, he placed the basket of pysanky in full view. He began to doodle, and pretty soon it became a dragon. The dragon was in a cage, and the cage was hung with pysanky; the dragon was smiling. And so was Andy.

And so was Edie when she met Andy at the door the following Tuesday. "Oh, Andy, the most marvelous thing has happened. Harry—he's my husband—and I got invited to your sister's wedding. Will you come with me this afternoon to pick out a wedding present? What do you think she would like?"

"A ninety-day flea collar."

"She doesn't need that. Even if Mary Jane had a dog, it would never have fleas."

"She really needs a good, swift . . ."

"Sh, sh, sh," Edie said. "Don't say it. We'll find it together."

Edie was not difficult to shop with. She looked fast and decided fast. But nothing seemed right until they reached the second floor of Dalton's. There they came upon a display of art needlework and a sign saying:

"Andy, Andy, that's it," Edie exclaimed. "That is absolutely it." She pointed to the sign, and Andy read it. "We don't have time to wait for Mr. Morgan LaFay, but we don't need him. I'll buy the blank canvas now, and you'll draw on it, and I'll do the needlepoint. I'll give Mary Jane a needlepoint pillow for her wedding present."

"I only do dragons."

"Of course that's all you do. And that is just what Mary Jane needs. She should have a dragon to start her marriage off right, don't you think?" Andy shrugged. "Well, look at how she's such a nerd without one."

"Did you call Mary Jane a nerd?" Andy wasn't sure what a nerd was, but it sounded as if it fit Mary Jane.

"A nerd is a nonperson. A person without dragons. We'll just have to give her a dragon, Andy."

So they bought a blank canvas and chose yarns in the colors of their garden, plus black, because you can't think "dragons" without some black.

* * * *

Andy had not finished drawing the dragon by

56

DESIGNED BY,
ANDREW J. CHR.
Needlepointed by,
Ms. E. Yakots

57

Thursday, but they didn't want to disappoint Sister Henderson, so they drove to her house from Emerson.

She came skipping and bouncing to the car, the least dignified Andy had ever seen her look.

"You seem cheerful today," Edie said.

"Ah got good news fo' me. Fo' me an' Brother Banks. We be delighted that you dint box that sixty-three. Thirty-six hit." She chuckled. "'Magine hitting that fo' five dollahs."

"Oh, well," Edie said, "as long as Brother Banks was pleased."

Andy was confused. He didn't know why Sister Henderson referred to boxing sixty-three. The gift had only been for five dollars. But he didn't want to ask. It wasn't cool to show too much curiosity. And sometimes it was not considered polite.

Edie had finished with Sister as quickly as possible so that Andy could complete the drawing of the dragon. She zigged and zagged, in and out of the detour around St. Vincent's. The needlework would take a lot of time, and she wanted to get it started. Edie was almost as enthusiastic about the dragon pillow as she was about their garden. Andy leaned back in the car. Besides being a neat driver, Edie was an interesting sidekick/person. In private.

CHAPTER EIGHT

The following Thursday they zoomed over to Sister Henderson's again. In and out of the detour and straight up to her porch. They again wanted her to finish as quickly as possible. There was still much work to do on Mary Jane's pillow. But Sister was not ready. She was usually on the front stoop waiting for them, but today she was not. They waited in the car for a few minutes and discussed whether or not they ought to honk the horn. They thought that doing so would not set the good example they wanted to set for manners in the ghetto. Andy decided that he would walk to the front door and knock. Or he would ring the bell if they had them in the ghetto.

The screen door was closed. (No one in Foxmeadow had screen doors. Some homes had windows that couldn't open. In Foxmeadow everything was air-conditioned except the jock things: the golf course, the tennis courts and the swimming pool.) Andy pressed his face against the screen (it left graph paper on his nose) and saw the whole inside of Sister Henderson's house. She was sitting in the living room. He guessed that it was the living room even though there was a dining room table in it, right across from the sofa. She was watching out of a side window. She was so intent on looking at whatever she was seeing that she answered his hello without taking her eyes from the window. "Hey, Andy, how 'bout you an' Miz Yakots comin' on in for a cup a Coke 'fore we start?"

So, thought Andy, they drink Coke from a cup in the ghetto. "But, Sister Henderson," he said, "we'd like to finish before three if that's at all possible."

"C'mere, Andrew," Sister Henderson said. Andy walked over to the window, and Sister pointed. "See that gray Plymouth restin' down the road a piece? That ain't no ornary car. That car means gray evil. That man behine th' wheel is waitin' for *me*. He be waitin' for me to colleck, then the minute Ah be finished, he'll grab me, and there'll go mah donations for the entire week."

Robbers! Andy thought. Robbers! Robbers! At last.

He felt his heart begin to pound. He had to play it cool. Robbers were not as good as murderers to catch, but they were a start. The important thing, the most important thing, was to play it cool. He'd better not tip off Yakots, and he'd better just stay cool. If he hinted anything at all to Yakots, she would panic and ruin everything. He would take it one step at a time. Coolly. The first step was to get Sister Henderson out to the car. It was a sure thing that he would catch no crooks with her staying inside the house. She was the bait, and the crooks were the prey, and he would be the trap. He liked that thought, so he repeated it to himself. Sister was the bait, the crooks were the prey, and he was the trap. He didn't exactly know how the trap would work, but first he had to give his prey the scent of his bait. He liked that thought, too.

He looked back out the window and said to Sister Henderson, "You say that the gray Plymouth is gray evil, then I say that the Devil is driving. He's trying to undo the good church work you do. That's the Devil, Sister, and I say that the Devil is driving a gray Plymouth today."

Sister Henderson looked up at Andy with interest. Andy could hardly control the excitement in his voice. But he was determined to stay cool. And he felt that he had to talk very slowly to her. He had been brilliant so far. "Mrs. Yakots understands the work of the Devil. She is quite familiar with dragons, and I am known as the dragon master of Emerson Country Day School. Now, let us, you and me, go out to the car, and challenge that Devil."

"There's two in that car," Sister said.

Andy looked out the window again. He had been so busy thinking about traps and bait that he had allowed his powers of observation to slip. "Yes, well, those two Devils."

Sister Henderson gathered together her purse and her first bag. Andy was surprised that he had been as persuasive as he had hoped to be. It made him a little nervous to think about it, and that wasn't helping his cool.

"Miz Yakots, thass a lady Ah c'n count on," Sister Henderson said as she closed and locked the door behind her.

"What took so long?" Edie asked when they got to the car.

"Just get this heap moving, Yakots. We'll discuss it later."

"Sure, boss," Edie said, and she pulled away from the curb, into Rutgers Avenue.

Andy tried to keep his eyes front, but he could not resist. He looked behind and saw that the gray Plymouth had pulled out when they had. He tried to keep his eyes forward, but he could not.

"What do you keep looking back for?" Edie asked.

Sister Henderson did not give him a chance to answer. "We might catch some trouble today, Miz Yakots. There's always the Devils to pay, and today they 'pears to be ridin' in that ole gray Plymouth."

Andy would have liked to pull the steering wheel out from the front and give it to Sister as a hat. A hard hat. He was furious. Couldn't she keep her mouth shut, for God's sake? Now Edie wouldn't stay cool, and now his big chance to catch some crooks would be all messed up even before he had a chance to think of how he would set the trap. "Listen, Yakots," Andy said, "just stay on Rutgers until you have to turn off at the hospital. We'll take our regular route to Sister Coolidge's. Our regular route, do you hear, Yakots? Now stay cool and take our regular route. Our regular route right to Sister Coolidge's. You're not telling me if you're hearing me, Yakots."

"You don't give me a chance, boss. I can hear you."

"Now, what did I say that you were supposed to do? Let's hear it, Yakots."

"I'm supposed to stay on Rutgers until the detour and take our regular route to Sister Coolidge's."

"Aha! See, Yakots? I said stay on Rutgers until the hospital."

"That's where the detour is, boss."

"Well, yes. But I was just checking your listening. Now, stay cool, Yakots, and drive."

When they stopped at the red light just before the detour, Andy saw a van carrying eight portable toilets start to pull out. It straightened out and took its place in the line of traffic, just in back of them. There was now the van and one other car blocking a clear view of the Plymouth. The crooks might lose sight of them, too, and then they wouldn't start anything, and then he couldn't catch them. There was a clear stretch just beyond the detour, and the cars seemed anxious to make up for the delay caused by the construction. They zoomed down the open boulevard. Edie did the same, and Andy was furious. The van carrying the Port-A-Lets had to shift gears and couldn't make as fast a getaway. There was a half block distance between them and the van, which meant that there was that distance plus the distance of one additional car between them and the gray Plymouth. Just as the van was catching up with them, Edie jammed on the brakes. The van carrying the Port-A-Lets did the same, stopping only inches from them. The portable toilets were jerked loose, and two of them fell off the truck and landed on the street. Three others had sloshed forward and were dripping all over the back of the truck. Magnolia Boulevard had suddenly become the largest outdoor bathroom in Gainesboro.

Every bit of traffic behind the truck was delayed. Every bit, including the gray Plymouth.

"Well, boss," Edie said, "we'll make it home by 3:15 after all. Mary Jane's dragon needs some flowers, I think."

"So do Magnolia Boulevard," Sister Henderson said, chuckling.

Andy said, "Listen, Yakots, I expected to outsmart those crooks, not outhouse them, for God's sake."

"Well, Andy," Edie answered, "we don't have time for any dragons except Mary Jane's today."

"You be right, Andrew," Sister Henderson said. "You be very right. Miz Yakots do unnerstan' dragons."

CHAPTER NINE

Edie wanted to have Mary Jane's dragon finished—stuffed and ready—on the Friday before the wedding. By Thursday there was still work to be done, but they had to take time out again. Andy had asked Edie if she were going to use foam rubber or dacron to stuff the dragon, and Edie had replied, "Not a wedding-gift pillow. They're stuffed with rice, some laurel for smell and a penny for luck."

"If she doesn't decorate her sofa with it, she can feed it to the birds."

"Oh, I hope not," Edie said. "They can get copper poisoning from the penny, I think. Maybe. Maybe birds don't."

Sister Henderson was waiting on the corner of Rutgers and Magnolia Boulevard, the very intersection where the Port-A-Let van had pulled in back of them the week before. Sister flagged them down with her umbrella. She scooted into the back seat and said, "Best go to Brother Folk's place first. He say that he gone haf to carry his auntie to the throat doctor 'long 'bout now. Best we start with him and run the run backward this week."

"But, Sister Henderson," Edie protested, "that's so roundabout, and we have to finish the needlepointing before we can do the stuffing."

"Won' take too much extra time, an' doin' it this-away may jus' save me from doin' lotsa time later. Nex' week, I figgers we be back to normalcy. It's in the springtime that the Devil rise wit' the sap. It happen every year."

After they finished their duly appointed (backward) rounds, they headed toward Brother Banks's house. As Edie slowed down and signaled that she was about to make the right-hand turn onto the dirt road that led to Banks's house, Andy spotted a car coming toward them. It wasn't Brother Maytag's. It was the gray Plymouth. As the car passed theirs, he saw two men. The man beside the driver rubbernecked to see into Edie's car as they passed. Edie was concentrating on making her turn and seemed not to notice.

Andy was convinced that the car was the one which had followed them the week before (the Devil's car). He wondered if Sister Henderson had noticed it. He wanted to ask, but he didn't want to arouse Edie's suspicions. He looked back at Sister Henderson, raised his eyebrows and rolled his eyes in the direction of the Plymouth. Sister nodded. Andy put his finger over his mouth, indicating to her to say nothing.

Sister Henderson could not read sign language. At least not normal, nonghetto sign language. Because he had no sooner signaled her to be quiet than she blurted out, "Y'know, Andrew, Ah done tole Brother Banks a lot 'bout you. He be anxious t' meet you. Howdja like t' carry the donations on to his place here this afternoon? While you doin' that, Miz Yakots an' me c'n run down to the Minute Market an' pick me up some aspurn. Ah feels a mos' appropriate long headache comin' on."

Edie said, "I'll take the donations in to Brother Banks."

Sister Henderson looked astonished, "Then who gonna drive me fo' mah aspurn?"

"That's right," Edie said. Then turning to Andy she added, "I'll buy the rice for the dragon while Sister is buying her aspirin."

Andy got out at the end of the drive leading to Brother Banks's house. He walked down the dusty, unpaved path and wondered how, for God's sake, was a person expected to stay cool in all this heat? And how was a guy expected to look cool carrying all these dumb-sized, awkward paper bags? Before he had reached the end of the drive, Sister Henderson poked her head out of the window and yelled, "Ah thinks Ah'll take a bus ride to home from the Minute Market. Bes't' tell Brother t' hol' up mah part."

Andy continued walking down the drive. "Got that, Andrew?" she yelled.

Andy turned and gave Sister a haughty look. "No one has to repeat things to me. I am trained. The only thing I didn't hear is *please*."

"Tell Brother I say to *please* hol' mah part 'til nex' week."

"It's me you should be saying please to, for God's sake."

"You min' yo' manners, son. Don' you go takin' the name of the Lawd in vain."

"You telling me to mind my manners is like the pot calling the kettle black . . ." Andy said, ". . . but of course that's perfectly all right. Black is beautiful."

"Now, jes' you tell him to hol' mine, y'hear?" Sister Henderson then turned to Edie and said, "Once he in the house, he be safe. Once he outta the house an' empty-handed, I be safe. Now, Miz Yakots, let us move us to the Jacksons' Minute Market."

Andy walked across the porch and knocked on the screen door. That made the second screen door within two weeks that he had looked through. He couldn't see much; there wasn't much to see. A man yelled, "C'min," and Andy did.

"Are you Brother Banks?" he asked.

"Been that for fifty-four year jes' las' Monday gone," the man answered.

"I've got Sister Henderson's donations," Andy said.

"Whassa matta with Sista? Why she don' bring her own?" A different man asked that. He was sitting behind an old kitchen table that had an adding machine on it.

Andy winked. The two men stared at him. He winked again and smiled. They still did nothing to show they understood. Oh, for God's sake, if they couldn't under-stand a cool signal like that, he'd just have to tell them. "The gray Plymouth," he muttered out of the side of his mouth.

The man behind the adding machine said, "Speak out,

plain, boy. This may be a checkup house, but don' take it personally. Nobody checkin' up on you. You c'n tell us straight out."

"The men in the gray Plymouth are trying to hold Sister up. She led them to the Minute Market where they won't cause trouble. Then Mrs. Yakots will come back to pick me up."

The man behind the adding machine said to Brother Banks, "Some pickup lady you got. She be pickin' up childern and troubles."

Brother Banks answered, "Don' go faultin' Sista. She be one a the best. She be wary." Brother Banks then began opening the bags. They were full of paper slips and coins and some paper money, nothing bigger than a one. He made a neat pile of the crumpled slips and handed them to the other man who began totaling them on the adding machine. Then Brother Banks started counting the money, sliding one or two coins to the edge of the table and letting them drop into his palm. "Four twenty-two, four forty . . ,"

"What church do you belong to?" Andy asked.

"Church?" Brother Banks looked up, holding an index finger on top of the quarter he was ready to count. "Church of God," he answered. "Four forty . . ."

"No," Andy corrected. "That would be four sixty-five. You're past four forty."

"How you know, son?"

"I'm trained. Trained myself. I count a lot of things. All churches are churches of God. Which one is yours?"

"Which one of what be mine?"

"Which church of God are you minister of?"

"The Church of God's Good Fortune. Four eighty . . ."

"Nope," Andy corrected again. "You're still at four sixty-five. You counted that quarter, but didn't palm it yet. Are you a Holy Roller? I mean in God's Good Fortune? I have heard that a lot of Blacks are Holy Rollers."

"Ah'll tell you what," Brother Banks answered. "When a seven comes up on my very first roll, Ah say that Ah *am* a Holy Roller." He looked back down at the table and said, "Four eighty." His eyes rolled up toward Andy. Andy nodded yes, and Brother Banks continued, "Five dollahs an' thirty."

Andy didn't interrupt further. He looked around the room. It was almost bare. In one corner he noticed a stack of newspapers. All the *New York Times*. He wandered over to the stack, looked through them and noticed that they were all Friday editions. While he glanced through the papers, Brother Banks and his friend talked to each other. The man behind the adding machine rolled some bills together and wound them around with a rubber band. He tossed the roll to Andy. Andy tossed it back.

"Too hot for you?" he asked.

"No," Andy answered, "but if that's your contribution to Sister Henderson, she said to hold it for her."

The two men looked at each other and shrugged. "That's what she said," Andy repeated. They said nothing, and Andy didn't know whether or not he was supposed to leave. To cover his awkwardness he said, "Well, it was nice meeting you two." They still said nothing. Andy felt himself begin to blush. "It's nice to meet someone who reads the *New York Times* right here in Gainesboro. My mother, now, my mother likes to read the book reviews in the *New York Times*. She says that it saves her from having to read the books. That's what my mother says. Of course, she says it about the Sunday *Times* mostly." The men folded their arms across their chests, both of them staring at Andy and saying nothing. But they were smiling. Andy cleared his throat. "Now, as for the local paper, I prefer the Thursday edition. It's got more in it in the way of ads, paper towels and stuff." They still said nothing. "Uh," Andy said, "what do you most enjoy about the newspaper?"

The man behind the adding machine folded his arms across his chest, tilted back on his chair and said, "When it comes to newspapahs we mostly enjoys the *New Yo'k Times* Friday editions. What we mostly enjoys has mo' t' do with makin' book than with readin' them. Now, you tell Sistah Hendahson that nex' week she to bring huh own. Y'heah, son? You tell that t' Sistah when you sees huh. Now, so long t' you an' don' forget t' tell Sistah like Ah tole you."

"Well, then, so long," Andy said. He waved limply, not cool. He walked down the steps and waited for Edie on the porch. But he wasn't comfortable there. He decided to walk to the main road to meet her. She seemed to be taking an awful long time. A normal sidekick would be a better judge of time, using as a measure all the other times they had stopped at Brother Banks's. As he walked, he kicked the dust in the rut. He was walking and kicking and thinking when the oleander that lined the sides of the road parted, and a man jumped into his path.

"Hold it a minute, son," the man said. He stood spread-eagled across the path. He lifted his chin, keeping his eyes on Andy. The oleander on the other side of the path parted, and a second man appeared. This one stood behind Andy.

Andy was furious. How could such a cool, tough detective-in-(high) training get himself caught in such a primitive trap? "Whadya want?" he snarled. His heart was pounding; his eyes seemed to have suddenly developed blisters, and something was hammering at his head from the inside. Everything was hot, very, very hot.

"Take it easy, fella," the first man said. "We would just like for you to empty your pockets."

"A man's pants are his castle. You got a search warrant?"

"Listen, kid, suppose you just tell us what you carried into that house."

At that moment the man turned. Edie had raced into the road from the highway, her horn blasting. She pulled to a screeching halt, just pennies short of hitting the first man. She opened the door to the car, jumped out and yelled *Catch!* at the same time as she threw a five pound sack of rice toward him. The man turned and held out his arms and caught it. She leaned back into the car, took out a second five pound sack, yelled *Catch!* again, and the second man did the same. While they were clutching the stuffings of Mary Jane's pillow, Andy used the time to dive toward the car and get in. Edie didn't give the men a chance to have even first thoughts about what they would do with their catch. She got into the car a second behind Andy, shifted into reverse and zoomed out of the drive, like a comic motion picture run backward.

"Well, boss," Edie said after they were safely driving in the right-hand lane of the Interstate, "how'd we do?"

"Aw, for God's sake, Edie, you go around acting like a rough and tough mess-'em-up kind when I expect to be cool. I was handling everything perfectly all right. I had told them that a man's pants are his castle and . . ."

"Those guys had guns, Andy."

"Oh, sure. Yeah. Yeah. Sure they did."

"I saw them."

"Well, that doesn't make sense. You were there just a second, and I was there longer, and I am a trained observer."

"Actually, I didn't know until they caught the rice. And actually, I didn't see the guns."

"Aha! It is dangerous to jump to conclusions, Yakots. Very dangerous. Besides, a sidekick isn't supposed to make conclusions, let alone jump to them."

"They had guns, all right. They were in shoulder straps or harnesses or whatever they're called."

"Oh, those straps. I noticed those. They were under their jackets. I thought it was funny that they should wear suspenders when they had belts, too. My father only wears suspenders when he wears a tuxedo." Andy fell back against the seat and whistled. "For God's sake," he said. And that was the last thing he said until they pulled up in front of his house, and he said, "So long, Yakots."

CHAPTER TEN

I f Andy's nerves were bad that evening at supper, no one
noticed. Because everyone's nerves played second
string to Mrs. Chronister's. She came to the supper
table with her nerve endings hanging out like a box of
moist excelsior that had suddenly been opened and
allowed to dry. Every day closer to the wedding it got
worse. As of that Thursday, Mrs. Vivian J. Chronister of
8129 Serena Road, Foxmeadow, Gainesboro had 4,326
extra feet of nerve endings that no one could stuff back
into her five-foot-four-inch frame.

"The caterers are coming tomorrow," Mrs. Chronister
began. She didn't even wait for the preliminaries: *And how
was your day, dear? Just delicious, and how was yours?* It was like
starting a basketball game without singing "The Star-
Spangled Banner," for God's sake. "The caterers are coming,
and so are the tent makers. The caterers are going to set up
the tables, and the tent makers are going to set up the tent."

"The detectives will be coming also," Mr. Chronister
said. "Everyone can take a tour of the premises together.
You can have a preparty party."

"Detectives?" Andy asked. "What do you need detectives for, for God's sake?"

"To guard the gifts and the furs."

"What furs? In May, for God's sake?"

"Many of our guests will be wearing fur wraps. It gets chilly in air conditioning. Your father, at my suggestion, has hired two off-duty city detectives to guard them."

"Why do you need the fuzz to guard the furs when you've got me? I'm going to be a detective."

"But," said Mr. Chronister, "you will be busy with our guests. You and I must be gracious hosts."

"If the people that you have invited are our friends, then why do you have to guard against them?"

"Oh," Mrs. Chronister said, "whatever made you think that a person invites only friends to a wedding? Heaven knows, we had to invite relatives, too, and we have as many of your father's business acquaintances and clients coming as we have friends. Besides, this wedding has had so much publicity in the society columns that everyone knows our place will be as loaded with jewelry as a bank vault. It would take only one carload of crooks to fleece everyone who comes to dinner. Old Tim Feagin wouldn't know a carload of crooks from a carload of your father's relatives. And we can't ask him to check everyone to see if he has an invitation. We wouldn't want our guests to feel that we don't trust them."

"What I want to know," Mary Jane said, "is how we're going to fit in two odd males? Two men no one will know. Where will the caterer seat them?"

"Now, that's the last thing that you have to worry about," Mr. Chronister explained. "They won't look odd at all. No one will know that they're here. One will help park the cars; he'll keep an eye on things on the outside. The other will be dressed as a waiter; he'll keep an eye on things on the inside, the furs, the guests and the wedding gifts."

Andrew could stand it no longer. He exploded. "Do you mean to tell me that you hired two detectives when you have me, Andrew Jackson Chronister, available? What kind of parents are you, showing no faith in your son? Your son who has been in training for months and months and practically a year?" He glared at his father. "I'm sitting out this whole wedding."

"That's fine with me," Mr. Chronister said, "providing that you sit it out first at the church and then very quietly here at home. And that you smile while sitting it out."

Andy left the table in disgust. His fury at his father was piled on top of his rage at Yakots. What kind of a sidekick saved a cool, tough detective by throwing five pounds of rice and yelling *Catch!* Not once but twice. No human being could be expected to survive as much heat as he felt. He would have to ditch Yakots. He would have to ditch his father, too. Someday. After he had finished Emerson, high school, and college.

Why would his father hire two detectives when he already had Andy? He could easily handle security at the wedding. He could recognize a shoulder holster now. He could tell one even if the person were also wearing a tuxedo and suspenders.

Of course, when he was famous, he wouldn't have to be involved with rough-'em-up types. He would just make appointments to solve famous but dignified murders.

He went up to his room and saw the pysanky on his desk. He took the basket and put it in the trash. Very carefully. Then he took down a piece of drawing paper and drew dragons. He drew (maybe) a hundred dragons, all chasing each other around the page and off it. In one corner a dragon was sitting at a table eating (supper) and in another corner two were driving a car. He colored the car gray.

Andy stopped at Edie's the next day after school, even though he usually didn't on Fridays. He had thought about it the whole night and the whole morning and the whole day at school, and he had to do something. He would give her back the Easter eggs. (He had taken them out of the wastepaper basket the night before, immediately after he had made up his mind. Or maybe immediately before.) Today he would tell Edie that she was dismissed. He would go it alone for a while. He would return the pysanky. Edie would be fired, and that would be that. After all these weeks she still had no idea of what a cool detective really did. Or how a side-kick worked. He certainly didn't need her talking about life and art and dragons instead of helping with his train-ing. Even though sidekicks weren't supposed to help with the training, they certainly weren't supposed to dis-cuss life and art and dragons. And he certainly didn't need her yelling *Catch!* and leaping into cars and making him follow. Of course he had had to follow; how else could he have gotten home?

Edie answered the door and began talking a stream. "I bought more rice, and I stayed up until two o'clock in the morning finishing. And laurel is bay leaves, so I bought some at the same store I got the rice, and I found a penny from the year that Mary Jane was born, and do you want to hold or pour?"

"I want to talk to you."

"Sure, Andy," Edie said. She dropped everything and sat with her hands folded across her lap, ready to listen. "What do you want to talk about, boss?"

"This business of your being my sidekick."

"Yes?"

"Well, you're ruining my reputation as a cool detective."

"I thought that a person had to *have* a reputation before he got it ruined."

"That may be so," Andy replied, "but if you insist on being the punch-'em-up, fast getaway, *Catch!* type, I can't go along with it. My style is to be cool and smooth. You can't solve a mystery if you don't stay cool."

"But you can't find one if you do," Edie answered. "You have to find the mystery before you can solve it. Sometimes finding it is all there is. Sometimes you never solve it."

"That's not so. I'll be the one detective who can."

"Maybe," Edie said, "but I doubt it. You're trying to be a detective for the same reason that I started carrying

Sister Henderson. We're both looking for the same thing. We're both on the same trail, but I know where I'm going."

"Just where are you going?"

"Right now, I'm going into the kitchen to clean this penny with copper cleaner. I think it's much nicer to put a shining penny into a wedding pillow. Will you pour?"

"I came here to fire you."

Edie said, "Later."

So Edie held the bag, and Andy poured the rice into the pillow after she had put in the penny and the laurel. "I'll have it all sewn up and wrapped before Harry—he's my husband—comes home, and I'm married again. We'll be there tomorrow, and I can hardly wait. Andy, will you please carry the dragon over to your house? Just put it with the other presents that have arrived today. I have a card all signed and ready. I know that I'll say everything wrong if I deliver it. I got a new dress for the party, and Harry—he's my husband—says that I look as normal as gooseberry pie. Actually, that's quite a compliment because people usually say 'as normal as blueberry pie.'" She bit off the thread as she finished the final seam, and she smiled up at Andy. "I can't believe that I'm going. It's my first big party since we moved here."

Here was Edie Yakots, a grown-up person, excited and nervous, too nervous even to take a present over to the house. She had bought a new dress for a wedding that wasn't even hers. Everyone else in Foxmeadow, except Mrs. Chronister and Ms. Chronister, he was sure, would wear something that they had worn to the Debutante Ball or to the Foxmeadow Frolics. "For God's sake," Andy told her, "Mary Jane is more cool about her very own wedding than you are."

"Oh, yes," Edie agreed. "That's why Mary Jane needs a dragon." Andy looked puzzled. "Not that I believe that you can ever really give anyone a dragon. Everyone has to find his own. But it doesn't hurt to try. Especially when they're not even looking. I guess it is mostly when you know that someone is looking for a dragon that you should not give it to him. Just try to help him find it."

The pillow was awkward. Well, Andy thought, dragons were awkward. They had to wrap it in tissue paper because Edie wrapped it raw, without a box, and normal gift wrap wouldn't work. They had used tissue paper of primary colors: red, yellow and blue. Well, Andy thought, dragons were primary. He carried the present up to Mary Jane's room. Andy thought that if they recycled all the gift wrap there, it would make enough Coca-Cola cartons for seven years of drought. Edie's was the only gift not wrapped in white. For a wedding present it looked as normal as gooseberry pie. Well, Andy thought, dragons were as normal as gooseberry pie.

He'd have to fire Edie later. After the weekend. After Mary Jane's marriage.

CHAPTER ELEVEN

Andy was made to sit in the front row of seats, those reserved for members of the family. He kept turning around to see who was coming in. Edie arrived early. She looked different. Maybe because he had never seen her out of context. Like once he saw his first-grade teacher in the supermarket, dressed in shorts, for God's sake. He hadn't known what to do, so he had ducked down one aisle after another until they ran into each other (cart to cart) at the ice-cream counter, and Andy had been so taken aback that he had saluted.

Edie didn't wave at Andy at all. He had expected her to carry on insanely when she spotted him; he had made up his mind that he wouldn't pay any attention, that the minute he spotted her, he would keep his eyes on his lap. But he kept looking back at her to catch her eye. But he couldn't. She looked at everyone coming down the aisle. Maybe Harry—her husband—had warned her about behaving. She looked different. Then Andy realized that she was not wearing her glasses. She probably couldn't see him. He'd help. He twisted around in his seat and waved

his hand until he caught Harry—her husband's—attention. Harry smiled and gently tapped Edie and pointed to Andy. Finally, Edie herself waved. Andy sat around in his seat, staring ahead and realizing that he had been waving like an antenna in a high wind, for God's sake.

The ceremony took too long. Mary Jane was not satisfied with simply walking down the aisle and having the minister say things to her and to Alton. She had had to put in her two cents, too. She said poetry to Alton, and he said some to her. And then they both said the same things at the same time to the minister. None of them were things they had made up. They were memorized from some book that was not the Bible. Andy looked back at Edie to exchange a smirk with her, but there was no chance of catching her eye. She was smiling and squeezing Harry—her husband's—hand. And she had put on her glasses. She wasn't missing one single thing except Andy's smirk. She could have seen Andy if she had wanted to, if she weren't concentrating so hard on the ceremony.

After the part in the church, everyone who was in the wedding party or who was a member of the family went to the Chronisters' house and formed a line. The guests walked past the line one by one. Most of them shook hands with everyone, but a lot of them kissed everyone, and after seven minutes, Mr. Chronister looked as if he had a case of terminal poison ivy. But he smiled and took it; he took it all: Revlon, Estee Lauder, Max Factor and Yardley.

When Harry and Edie Yakots walked through the

receiving line, they shook hands with everyone. Until Edie got to Andy. She had taken her glasses off again, and she was starting to shake hands with him before she noticed that the short person whose hand she was shaking was her boss, Andy. When she did, it was *sayonara* for Andy. She hugged him.

"Oh, boss," she said. "I'm so glad we came. And there's more to come, and it was so already beautiful."

After the Yakotses had passed the whole length of the receiving line, Mr. Chronister turned his decorated face to his son and asked, "Who was that wild woman? One of your mother's relatives, I suspect."

"An impostor," Andy answered. "Why don't you have your two detectives arrest her?" That was all that Andy had a chance to say before he had to shake the next few hands.

As soon as they had passed through the line, the guests, each and every one, picked up a glass of champagne and began the real party. Andy figured that he had spent more time in line than any of the guests and that he deserved a glass of champagne more than any of them. So he helped himself. In that room crowded with friends, relatives, business associates, two detectives (somewhere) and one crazy lady named Edie Yakots, Andy drank alone. Everyone else was drinking toasts to Mary Jane and Alton; but Andy was toasting Andy.

His first glass of champagne tasted more like Alka-Seltzer than anything else. His second tasted like Alka-Seltzer with a dash of ginger ale. His third tasted like ginger ale altogether, and the fourth simply tasted wet. He lifted his fifth glass from the tray of the passing waiter. The waiter gave him a puzzled look; he gave the waiter a defiant look in return. His father took the glass from him and told him that it was time to eat.

Andy looked up at his father. His father was swimming. No, just his father's head was swimming. Andy thought that it was logical for his father's head to be swimming. How else could his father have washed himself clean of all those kisses? He smiled, pleased with his logic. His father seemed to be not smiling. He pulled Andy toward one of the round tables where he was to sit between Alton's brother and Alton's sister. He stared at the shrimp that was in place before him and wondered why shrimp that had been boiled, peeled and deveined should still be swimming. Through cocktail sauce. Andy looked at Alton's brother and Alton's sister. They were much older than he was. They looked old enough to have college or kids. It would be nice to ask them how old they really were, but he decided not to. No one could talk underwater. They weren't under as much water as his father had been. Their heads were just swaying with the tide like seaweed caught on a piling.

Andy next noticed his hands. He looked at them a very long time. He did not normally pay too much attention to his hands, but they were very heavy right now. That, too, was perfectly logical; his hands had absorbed all the weight from his head which was very light right now.

With the fat fingers of his right hand he managed to spear a shrimp. He smiled at it. Boy conquers fish. He bit a piece off, and it dried up, right inside his mouth. It wouldn't go down his throat because all of his breakfast and all of his lunch were suddenly there, clogging the passage. Andy put his napkin over his mouth and backed away from the table. He went upstairs to his room. He thought he walked up, but he couldn't be sure. His feet didn't remember touching the floor.

After he did what he had to do in the bathroom, he went to his own room. He lay down on his bed and watched the grate over the air-conditioner duct bend into various abstract shapes before the weight from his hands moved to his eyelids and forced his eyelids closed.

The lines of the air-conditioner grate were the last thing he focused on before he fell asleep (passed out). Noises coming from the air-conditioner grate were the first thing he focused on when he awakened (came to). Voices. Voices colored red and pale orange. Arguing voices. A man and a woman. No, two men and a woman: red, pale orange and a dash of sienna.

The woman ". . . because everyone forgot the rice."

Man One: "Now, lady, you can't make me believe that you came up here for rice. Rice is always kept in the kitchen in a nice house like this here."

The woman: "I just came for the dragon. It's full, and the bride is ready. It's instant because it weighs less."

Man Two: "Hold it a minute. You want us to believe that you are the only person at this whole party who knew that there was rice up here? You were throwing it around last Thursday."

The woman: "I wanted to surprise everyone who forgot the rice. Which was everyone. They all forgot the rice."

Andy's eyes wanted to go to sleep again, but some other sight, far in back of his eyes would not let him. The voices continued coming through the air conditioning. The woman's voice was Edie's of course. Who else would talk such nonsense to strangers? Two men strangers. Yet, not so strange. Their voices, their tone, were familiar. *Hold it a minute.* The men from the Plymouth. *Hold it a minute.* Last Thursday she was throwing it around. *Hold it a minute.* The waiter who had looked at him so strangely was one of the crooks. If the champagne bubbles had not gone to his brain, he would have realized who the man was before now. He could have tipped off his father. Where were his father's fine detectives now? He jumped off the bed. He had to rescue Edie. He'd rescue Edie and catch the crooks. Two missions in one. He would feel better about dismissing her after he had evened out the rescues.

If only his mouth were not so dry. He could think better if his tongue weren't drying out his brain.

He walked down the hall to Mary Jane's room. They had closed the door. The cheats! Couldn't trust a crook. He was closed out. He couldn't just turn the knob and walk in and request that they let Edie go. He'd have to be a rough-'em-up detective after all. Except that he was undersized and underarmed.

Underarmed! That was it.

He tiptoed past Mary Jane's room to the bathroom. In use! He had to go through his mother's and father's bedroom to get to theirs. There wasn't much time. He had to stay cool. He would find it easier to stay cool if only he weren't so thirsty. *Thirsty* made a guy hot.

The furs were piled high on his parents' bed. They looked like a giant hairy Moby Dick, for God's sake. Why weren't his father's famous detectives guarding the furs as they were supposed to? He had to do everything. All by himself. Someone was leaving his parents' bathroom just as he reached the door. "Lovely party," she said. Now, when he was busy being cool and committing a rescue, was no time for conversation. He gave his crotch a good tug, one that would have made Tim Feagin jealous, and he said, "Excuse me," as he brushed past the lady into the bathroom.

He didn't waste a minute; he didn't even take a drink of water, and God knows, he needed one. He reached inside the cabinet under the sink and took what he needed. He poked his head out the door, his very thirsty but cool head. The coast was clear. He walked rapidly, but coolly, down the hallway and turned the knob on the door to Mary Jane's room. Except that it didn't turn. Locked! The crooks had locked Edie inside. Cheats! He kicked at the door, leaving black scuff marks on the white paint. "Open up!" he yelled.

The instant he saw a crack of light through the door, he thrust one arm in and then the other. And he sprayed.

The man who came to the door got a shot of Arrid Extra Dry (unscented). Andy then kicked the door open the rest of the way and gave the other fellow a shot of Alberto VO Hair Spray, extra hold.

"Okay, Yakots, make a dash for it," he yelled.

"Oh, Andy," she answered, "how nice of you to come to my rescue."

"For God's sake, Edie, get a move on."

"You can help me straighten things out," Edie answered, still sitting.

The two crooks were coughing and sputtering. Andy turned to them and said, "Listen, you guys, get back against that wall, or you're going to get it again." The men moved. Andy was surprised that they listened so well. "Listen, Yakots, will you please move yourself out the door? I'm going to lock these guys in here and then get the detectives my father has hired. I'll do it quietly so as not to disturb the party going on downstairs."

"But, Andy . . ."

"Move, Edie. I don't have enough deodorant to hold these stinkers all day. Do you think I want to be this kind of detective in the first place? This isn't exactly my bag."

"That's what they want to know about, Andy. The bags."

"For God's sake, Edie. Will you please get my father? Tell him to send the detectives. But don't disturb any of the guests. Tell him dignifiedly. Nice and dignifiedly."

"Andy," Edie whispered, "these men . . ."

"I told you to tell *my father* quietly, Yakots. Now is not when you have to whisper. We're behind closed doors." He looked up at the first crook whose eyes were cleared now. He saw that the man was grinning. He didn't like the grin. "Listen, wise guy," Andy began. But he didn't finish. He wasn't supposed to be the kind of detective that said things like that.

"Andy," Edie said.

"What is it now, Yakots?"

"The first wise guy is one of the detectives your daddy hired, and the second one, the one blowing his nose, is the second one he hired."

"Hunh," Andy replied. "That just exactly shows you how much a smart man like my father knows about crime. He's gone and hired two crooks to guard furs and presents."

The man who had been blowing his nose coughed and said, "We're detectives from the police force. We were staked out at Brother Banks's last Thursday, and we tried to question you then. When we spotted Mrs. Yakots at this party, and we saw her sneaking up to the room with all the presents . . ."

"This one," Edie said, pointing to the one dressed as a waiter, "kept watching me and watching me and when all I wanted was our dragon back, he followed me. For the rice. Three boxes of instant. Except I only used about two and three-fourths. It's fluffier. Mary Jane and Alton were about to leave and no one remembered rice to throw for their honeymoon, fertility and all, so I decided to open the dragon. It would go pretty far, except I didn't. Get very far, that is. They followed me, and now I wonder if Mary Jane and Alton have left already. And it was such a pretty wedding."

Andy listened to Edie but watched the men. "Show me your identification," he demanded. They did. The man dressed as a waiter was Sergeant Piper, and the other man was Officer Feeling.

"Look," Edie pleaded, "if you let me open my dragon and give everyone some, I promise I'll come back and talk to you about the other bags."

Officer Feeling said to Sergeant Piper, "How do we know that she won't skip out?"

Edie answered, "I promise I'll come back. Harry—he's my husband—won't leave without me. And you don't see him here, do you?"

"But lady . . ."

"Let her throw the rice, for God's sake," Andy said. "She probably believes that Mary Jane's bottom will fall off tomorrow morning if you don't let her throw rice at it now."

"I don't know . . ."

"Listen," Andy said, "you've got me. I'll stay here as hostage."

Edie turned to Andy and said, "Thanks, boss." Then she looked at the two detectives and added, "I'm his side-kick." She started toward the door, turned the knob, thought a minute and said, "I'll throw a little something for you, boss."

"Yeah," Andy answered. "Hit her in the keester."

"Oh, I don't know if I can do that. You know I'm no jock. But I'll wear my glasses, just in case."

Andy wanted to disown her.

CHAPTER TWELVE

Edie returned to Mary Jane's room and Harry—her husband—came with her. Mr. Chronister followed Harry. And Mrs. Chronister, all chiffon and crying, followed Mr.

"They wanted to come along, boss," Edie said. "If I had worn my glasses the whole evening, I would have warned you, but it's hard to tell a waiter when you're hard of seeing."

Sergeant Piper said, "Now, why would she call you *boss* all the time if you are not her boss? We know that Brother Banks is not the real leader of the numbers racket here in Gainesboro. It wouldn't surprise me one bit to find some rich little kid doing something like that just for kicks."

"What is a numbers racket, for God's sake?" Andy asked.

"Gambling," Edie said. "Sister Henderson was picking up bets on numbers."

Officer Feeling asked Andy, "What did you think she was doing, running some kind of charity?"

"Exactly," Andy answered.

At that point Mr. Chronister took over. After all, he

was master of the house, employer of the detectives, father of the bride and one of the accused, and a lawyer besides. He first ordered Mrs. Chronister to control herself, and then he sent her back downstairs to say good-bye to the guests who might be ready to leave. He then asked each of the detectives to be seated. They sat on the edge of the bed, flanking Andy. Mr. Chronister pulled the chair from under Mary Jane's vanity and offered it to Mr. Yakots; he politely refused. He chose to remain standing in the doorway, the line of his arms folded across his chest repeating the line of his grin. Edie was left standing almost in the hall, clutching the dragon pillow like a punctured volleyball. Mr. Chronister nodded to her and motioned for her to enter. She obeyed. She made room for herself between Officer Feeling and Andy. Once seated, she raised her hand for permission to speak.

"Yes, Mrs. Yakots," Mr. Chronister said.

"I can explain," she volunteered.

"That would be most kind of you, Mrs. Yakots," Mr. Chronister said patiently, encouragingly. "Would you please proceed."

She cleared her throat, took a deep breath and began, "I went to the meeting of the Garden Circle because even though it's supposed to be good for your plants to talk to them, after a while they don't answer back." She paused and looked at Harry—her husband. He nodded, and she continued. "And the ladies there had more to say to each other than to me, so I looked at the pictures and saw Andy's dragon and right away I went to the secretary."

97

Mr. Chronister interrupted, "Can we back up a minute here, Mrs. Yakots?"

"Yeah," said Sergeant Piper, "what has Garden Circles and dragons to do with the numbers racket?"

Mr. Chronister gave Sergeant Piper a look that was enough to silence him. It was his best courtroom look. "Is that the dragon you were referring to, Mrs. Yakots?" he asked, nodding at the pillow that Edie had placed over her lap.

"No, this is the one for Mary Jane. It was a nice rice dragon, plump with rice, instant, until everyone forgot it, and I remembered the dragon, and I got caught."

Officer Feeling exploded, "What has dragons to do with Sister Henderson?"

Mr. Chronister asked Officer Feeling, "What, may I ask, has Sister Henderson to do with anything?"

Officer Feeling said, "This lady, this Mrs. Yakots, is a big woman for the biggest numbers racket in Gainesboro. Now, Mr. Chronister, if you'll give us just a minute, we think we can establish who is in charge of who. It just may be, sir, that your son, this Andrew, is the head of the whole collection scheme. You see, this lady, the one you call Mrs. Yakots, keeps calling your son *boss*. Now, it just may be that your son has decided to operate outside the law to give old dad a run for his money, something we know you have plenty of. He just may be doing it to embarrass daddy, or he may be doing it just for kicks. The pay isn't good enough to make it attractive to a rich kid. He's probably in it for kicks."

"And sidekicks," Edie said. "That's me."

Mr. Chronister looked grim. "Have you been collecting money for the numbers racket?" he asked Andy.

"I don't know," Andy answered. "We collect Sister Henderson, and she collects her donations."

"Those ain't donations," Officer Feeling said. "This Sister Henderson is picking up money from the numbers writers, and she takes it to Brother Banks who happens to run the checkup house. Banks pays her a commission on everything she picks up."

At that point Mr. Harry Yakots stepped inside the room and closed the door behind him. He walked over to his wife and stood looking down at her. His look was gentle, loving. "Looking for dragons, Edie?" he asked gently. She nodded yes. He patted her hand and looked up at the others in the room and said, "Let's pull this all together. Edie will tell what happened, and I'll interpret."

"Oh, Harry," Edie said, "that will be wonderful. Simultaneous translation. Just like the UN."

"Yes, dear," Harry said, "just like the UN."

Andy knew what Edie would have to say, but he didn't know all the details. She told how Sister Henderson had been in charge of the sale of the old church pews, one of which she had wanted to paint bright pink for her kitchen. When Edie had gone there to look them over, Sister Henderson had told her to hurry and make up her mind because she had to get the money over to Brother Banks's before three o'clock, which meant that she had to catch the city bus that left at 2:10. Edie volunteered to drive Sister Henderson over to Brother Banks's to deposit the money. Edie said (through Harry—her husband) that she had assumed that it was money from the sale. When they were in the car, Sister Henderson hinted at how she wished that she could have a ride every Thursday afternoon so that she could go to the houses for her collections instead of having to wait for people to bring them to her. Sometimes, she complained, they came so late that she was hard put to get to Brother Banks's by three. And that was how Edie had begun carrying Sister Henderson every Thursday. She had volunteered.

Sergeant Piper asked how Andy had come to be included in the pickups, and Edie through Harry—her husband—proudly explained about that. "Didn't it ever occur to you to ask where the money came from?" he questioned.

"I wondered," Edie said, "but when you're tracking dragons, there's a lot you're not supposed to understand."

Both the detectives looked at Harry to interpret that, but he didn't, so they turned to Andy. "And you, boy, didn't you ever wonder why all the money had to be in by three every Thursday?"

"Not at all," Andy answered. "When I collect for the Cancer Drive or for the Mothers' March Against Birth Defects or Kidneys or Hearts or Cystic Fibrosis, the money always has to be in by a certain time. I always have a deadline."

"Well, let me ask you about this. Do members of your church go around, house to house, to collect money?"

"No, the church doesn't. But the Cancer Drive, the Mothers' March Against Birth Defects, Kidneys, Hearts . . ."

"All right. All right," Officer Feeling said. "I get your point. But didn't it seem funny to you that church donations would be made on Thursday? Aren't church donations, most all church business, done on Sundays?"

"Now that," Andy said, "is easy to explain. I figured that everything that isn't the same in the ghetto is different. Like screen doors and Coke in a cup."

"Do you mean to tell me that you had no idea that you were accomplices in the numbers racket called Total?"

Andy said, "No idea." He felt as deflated as the dragon Edie held in her lap. He looked at Edie. Harry looked at her, too; he raised an eyebrow, in a cool gesture of inquiry. Edie looked up at him and shrugged.

The two detectives explained the operation of the illegal numbers lottery for which Sister Henderson had been picking up bets every Thursday. The lottery was called Total. Someone, anyone, could buy a chance on a number, any number from one to one hundred. They could bet five cents or five dollars, whatever they could afford (and very often what they could not afford). The person they buy the lottery ticket from is the numbers writer (Sister Coolidge, Brother Folk). Some people *box* their numbers, which means that if they bet on 45, they can also win if 54 hits. Boxed wins pay off less than straight hits. The pickup man or pickup lady (Brother Maytag, Sister Henderson) is assigned to a group of sellers. It is her duty on Thursday to go to each of the writers assigned to her (or meet them at a certain place) and pick up all the tickets that they had sold during the week. She also picks up the money. From there the pickup lady takes the tickets and the money to a checkup house (Brother Banks). Sister Henderson received 5 percent commission on all the money she brought in. ("Bes' t' tell Brother t' hol' up mah part.")

Andy asked, "How do they know what number wins? Do they pick it out of a hat?"

"Not in Total," Sergeant Piper said. "This operation is a Thursday lottery. They take the last two digits of the combined total of the liabilities of the twelve Federal Reserve Banks. That number is released to the *New York Times* at three o'clock on Thursday and is published in the paper in the Friday edition."

"That's why all the newspapers were Friday editions," Andy said. "When I asked Brother Banks and the other man, the one behind the adding machine, if they were interested in the book reviews, they said they were more interested in 'making books' than in reviewing them."

"'Making book' is another way of saying 'writing numbers,'" Officer Feeling explained. "Tell me about the man behind the adding machine," he urged.

Andy was quiet, and the wedding guests could be heard. They were coming upstairs, one, two at a time to collect their furs. Mr. Chronister excused himself; he had to be a proper host and say good-bye to his guests. Before he left he turned to his son and said, "Andy, you better tell these men all that you can about Sister Henderson and her donations. The illegal numbers lottery is taking money away from poor people who can't afford to gamble."

"Well," Andy protested, "it's giving jobs to some. Like Sister Henderson and Sister Coolidge and Brother Banks."

"Help them," Mr. Chronister commanded before he hurried downstairs to join his wife in saying farewell to their guests.

"About this man behind the adding machine," Officer Feeling said. "Can you give us a description?"

"Andy can do better than that," Edie said. "Andy can draw you a picture of him. Andy is an artist."

"I only draw dragons," Andy protested.

Edie looked at Andy and talked to him as if they were the only two people in the room; everything came out straight. "Now is the time to meet your dragon, Andy. Draw the man for him. You can do it. Now is the time, Andy. I know you can do it."

"Listen, Andrew," Sergeant Piper pleaded, "please help us. If you can give us some idea of who the man behind the adding machine was, we can track him down. It is your civic responsibility. We've staked out that place four times and can't get a glimpse of him."

"I only do dragons," Andy said.

Edie kneeled in front of Andy so that her eyes would be level with his. Andy looked away. "Look at me, Andy," she insisted. Andy did. "Draw the man for him. You can do it, Andy. Know your real dragon."

Someone, he wasn't sure who, handed him a pad and a ballpoint pen. "I can't draw with this," he said. "I need a

By,
Andrew J. Chr.

pen with wet ink." Someone brought him one. "This won't do either."

"What now?" Sergeant Piper asked, exasperated.

"The ink's blue. Black would be better."

"Draw. Draw, kid."

"Okay, for God's sake. But I won't guarantee it will come out right."

But it did. Andy drew a likeness of the man behind the adding machine, and once he got started, he dashed off a portrait of Brother Banks sitting beside him. It was an accurate drawing, one that would be as much help as fingerprints. Only a close observer would notice that the man's feet were unusual. Most people would think that Andy was trying to draw alligator shoes.

CHAPTER THIRTEEN

Everything was a letdown after the wedding. The papers carried headlines about the successful breakup of an important illegal numbers lottery. But Andy didn't get any credit. His father was a legal conservative; he had requested that Andy's name not be mentioned. He didn't want any crooks taking revenge on his son, the stool pigeon. Not that Andy wanted any credit anyway. Who wanted credit for that instead of for being a detective?

Everything else was wrong, too. He had participated in a crime instead of solving one. And he hadn't even known that he was participating. When he was finally called on to help, he hadn't helped in any analytical, cool, tough fashion. He had helped in an artistic one. All of his training to be an observer had only helped his drawing, after all. And another thing, who wanted to find out that Sister Henderson had been part of the numbers racket? He liked Sister. Her manners were not so good, but they weren't so bad either. She was the only black person he had ever thought about and really gotten to know. And she had that thing he really liked, that dignity. There was too much in the whole caper to feel bad about for him to feel good. When Sherlock or Ellery solved a crime, they had nothing at all to feel bad about.

School was over for the year only two weeks after the wedding. Andy avoided Edie every minute after school, and all the time when school was over. Thursdays seemed lonely; so did the other afternoons. But Thursdays especially. He tried to get involved with his analysis of the grocery ads, but he couldn't. He had never really enjoyed doing that anyway. Finally, he had only another week before he would go to camp (another ghetto, with a fence around it, too, for God's sake). At camp he was going to make an effort to be a jock. At camp and forever after.

In the meantime he had been doing a lot of drawing. He stayed in the house more than his mother considered healthy, but he insisted, and she gave in. She even bought him a set of oil paints. He painted in the utility room with the washer and dryer and the maid (in and out) for company. The first thing he painted in oils was a dragon. The second thing he did was a scene. Rutgers Avenue, all alive with people and construction trucks and sidewalks and traffic signals. It was both smoky and colorful.

In the middle of June, Mary Jane came home from her European honeymoon. She came to collect all her wedding gifts and move them into her new apartment. He watched. She put the limp dragon pillow into a plastic bag and layered it between the gift contour sheets and two sets of place mats. Andy asked her what she was going to do with it, and she told him that she would stuff it with foam rubber as soon as she got around to it.

But Andy knew she never would.

Andy knew that it would end up at a church bazaar or being given to the Salvation Army. Mary Jane had no room for dragons in her life. Her whole life was predictable. She would always be cool. She would never do anything foolish. There would be no discomfort in her life, and there would be no heroics either. She would always be a nerd. Dragons were what made life hard to live, yet no fun to live without.

He no sooner thought that than he realized that he needed dragons as much as Mary Jane did not. He needed some monster/mystery, some mystery/monster in his life. So did Edie.

Of course. Of course. Of course. For God's sake, of course.

The important parts of life were dragons: difficult, strange and awkward. He had been searching for mystery, for something uncertain, not crime. He had confused the two. Edie had understood. She had tried to help him. She had tried to help him find a crime so that he could realize that he didn't want it.

Maybe she had tried to help too much. Maybe she had known about Sister Henderson. Maybe. Maybe. Maybe, for God's sake, her conversation with Sister had been a code. *I like total involvement. As it says in the Bible about charity in Matthew, Chapter VI, verse three.* Total: that was the name of the game.

Andy ran downstairs and got a copy of the New Testament. He found Matthew VI:3. It said, "But when you give alms, do not let your left hand know what your right hand is doing." There! That verse was about charity. Alms *was* charity. Edie didn't know. But the same passage said not to let your left hand know what your right hand was doing. Edie did know; her right hand knew. Maybe.

He ran out of the house, straight to the Yakotses'. He rang the bell, and he hoped, he hoped, he hoped that someone would be home. And that it would be Edie. He had to find out about her. He would ask clever, leading questions and trap her into revealing whether or not she knew about Total.

Edie did answer the door. It was the first he had seen her since the wedding. "Hi, boss," she said.

"What's the matter with you, Yakots? You sure are losing your looks." That was not what he had meant to say at all. He had wanted to ask cool, leading questions. Then he remembered that he was done with being that kind of cool. Having a dragon and knowing how to live with it was the best cool. Edie Yakots, spacy, flaky Edie Yakots was the coolest person in Foxmeadow. What a relief! He could say whatever he wanted to. "You're getting fat, for God's sake." That's what he said.

Edie grinned. She said nothing.

He didn't have to be nonchalant. He could say anything else he wanted to. He could say it right out. "I know about dragons," he said.

Edie had walked into the kitchen and fixed them both Cokes. She had done Andy's with a maraschino cherry and with a swizzle stick and wrapped it with a napkin. He walked with it back into the living room. Edie sat down on the sofa under the dragon painting. "Come here," she said, patting the seat next to her on the sofa. Andy hesitated. But he walked over, carrying his glass and sat next to her. Edie said nothing but took his free hand and placed it on her stomach.

Andy was embarrassed. He hadn't seen her for a month, and here she was getting intimate. How could a guy stay cool, even if he knew that it was no longer necessary to stay cool?

Then he felt something bump. He jerked his hand away, and Edie laughed. Andy realized what Edie was trying to tell him, and he put his hand on her stomach again. He felt another bump. "Well, Yakots," he said, laughing, "now, that's what I'd call a real sidekick."

Edie took a sip from her glass of Coke and said, "Harry—he's my husband—was married before."

"I know all that, Yakots."

"So he already has someone named after him."

"So what's that mean?" Andy asked.

"So that means that we're thinking of naming him Andrew." She paused and ran her finger around the edge of her glass. "He'll know about dragons. Right from the beginning."

"Well," Andy said. "Well, well, well. Well," he said again. "Well!" He paused and laughed out loud. "Well,

Yakots, babies can be girls. What will you do if it's a girl?"

"Call her Andrea, I guess," Edie answered. "Either way, it'll be Andy. For short. For God's sake."

FORTY PERCENT MORE THAN EVERYTHING YOU WANT TO KNOW ABOUT E. L. KONIGSBURG

Hello, Mrs. Konigsburg.
Hello.

I thought that I might ask you some questions about your work and your life.
That's perfectly all right with me. I'll tell you everything except my age and weight.

Where do you live?
On the beach in North Florida. It's all right, isn't it, if I don't answer in complete sentences?

You're the writer, Mrs. Konigsburg. Let it be on your conscience. Do you have any children?
I have three. Their names are Paul, Laurie, and Ross. They have posed for the illustrations in my books. Laurie was Claudia and Ross was Jamie in *From the Mixed-up Files of Mrs. Basil E. Frankweiler*. Paul was Benjamin Dickinson Carr in *(George)*.

Do you have a husband?
Yes, I do, thank you. My husband's name is David, and he is a psychologist. Aren't you ever going to ask me about my books?

Patience. Patience.

I know I'm not supposed to ask you when you were born . . .
Ground rules. Ground rules.
. . . so I would like to ask you where you were born.
New York City. But we moved when I was still an infant. Except for a year and half when we lived in Youngstown, Ohio, I grew up in small towns in Pennsylvania. I graduated from high school in Farrell, Pennsylvania.

Did you always want to be a writer?
No. When I was in college at Carnegie Mellon University, I wanted to be a chemist, so I became one. I worked in a laboratory and went to graduate school at the University of Pittsburgh; then I taught science at a private girls' school. I had three children and waited until all three were in school before I started writing.

Where do you get the ideas for your books?
From people I know and what happens to them. From places I've been and what happens to me. From things I read. Do you have a specific book in mind that you would like to ask about?

All right. Where did you get the idea for *From the Mixed-up Files of Mrs. Basil E. Frankweiler?*
I had read in the newspaper that the Metropolitan Museum of Art in New York City had purchased a statue for $225. Even though they did not know who had sculpted it, they suspected it had been done by someone

famous in the Italian Renaissance. They knew they had an enormous bargain. (The statue is not an angel, and it was not sculpted by Michelangelo. It is called *Bust of a Lady*.)

The summer after that article appeared in the paper, our family took a trip to Yellowstone Park. One day, I decided that we should have a picnic. After buying salami and bread, chocolate milk and paper cups, paper plates and napkins, and potato chips and pickles, we got into the car and drove and drove but could not find a picnic table. So when we came to a clearing in the woods, I suggested that we eat there. We all crouched slightly above the ground and spread out our meal. Then the complaints began. The chocolate milk was getting warm, and there were ants all over everything, and the sun was melting the icing on the cupcakes. This was hardly roughing it, and yet my small group could think of nothing but the discomfort.

What, I wondered, would my children do if they ever decided to leave home? Where, I wondered, would they go? At the very least, they would want all the comforts of home, and they would probably want a few dashes of elegance as well. They would certainly never consider any place less elegant than the Metropolitan Museum of Art. How they love it! And how do I!

Yes, I thought, the Metropolitan Museum of Art. There they could surround themselves with elegance and enjoy the comfort of those magnificent beds. And then, I thought, while they were there, perhaps they could discover the secret of the mysterious bargain statue, and in doing so, they could also learn a much more important secret—how to be different on the inside where it counts.

That is all very interesting, Mrs. Konigsburg. How did winning the Newbery Medal for that book make you feel?
Proud and courageous.

Courageous? The Newbery Medal is an award for an outstanding contribution to children's literature. It is not given for courage. Are you getting your medals as mixed-up as your files?
Not at all. I'm not saying that I won the Newbery Medal for *having* courage; I'm saying that winning the Newbery Medal gave me courage. Let me explain. After I won the Newbery Medal, children all over the world let me know that they liked books that take them to unusual places where they meet unusual people. That gave me the courage to write about Eleanor of Aquitaine in *A Proud Taste for Scarlet and Miniver* and about Leonardo da Vinci in *The Second Mrs. Giaconda*. Readers let me know that they like books that have more to them than meets the eye. Had they not let me know that, I never would have written *The View from Saturday*.

I'm glad you brought up the subject of *The View from Saturday*. Why did you write that book the way that

you did—having four short stories right there inside the novel?

It was the most natural thing in the world. I had started writing a story about a young man named Ethan Potter who boards a school bus the first day of sixth grade. The bus takes an unexpected turn, and a strangely dressed young man boards and sits down next to Ethan. He introduces himself as Julian and explains that his father is about to open a bed and breakfast inn—*a B and B*. At that point, I left my desk and took a walk along the beach.

When I write a book, I more or less start a movie in my head, and there I was walking along the beach, doing a re-run of what I had written. When I got to where Julian was telling Ethan about the B and B, I remembered that I had a story in my files—my mixed-up files—about a young man named Noah whose mother insists that he write his grandparents a bread and butter letter, a B and B letter. Fact: That made me remember another short story I had about a dog named Ginger that plays the part of Sandy in the play *Annie*. And that led me to another story about an Academic Bowl team.

Fact: Before I had finished my walk, I realized that all those short stories were united by a single theme. Taken together, they reinforced one another, and the whole became more than the sum of the parts.

I knew that kids would love meeting one character and then two and three, and I also knew—because I had learned it from them—that they would think that fitting all the stories together was part of the adventure.

So how did you feel when you found out that you had won a Newbery Medal for *The View from Saturday*?
Filled with joy. And that's a fact. I knew I had been right about the spirit of adventure shared by good readers.

Do you have any hobbies?
I love to draw and paint. I love to read and walk along the beach. I also love movies.

What makes you feel bad?
Eating too much chocolate, reading trash, and letting dust balls gather under the sofa.

What makes you feel good?
Eating too much chocolate, reading trash, and letting dust balls gather under the sofa.

Really, Mrs. Konigsburg, will you try to be serious?
I am very serious about chocolate.

Let's get back to your books.
I am very serious about those, too.

People tell me that your books don't always appear to be serious.
I consider that a compliment. Thank you.

I guess that's about all I had to ask. I don't know how to end this interview.
Try saying "Thank you."

Thank you, Mrs. Konigsburg.
You're welcome, Mrs. Konigsburg.

BOOKS BY E. L. KONIGSBURG ⎯

Jennifer, Hecate, Macbeth, William McKinley, and Me, Elizabeth
0-689-30007-7 **Atheneum**
Newbery Honor Book
ALA Notable Children's Book

From the Mixed-Up Files of Mrs. Basil E. Frankweiler
0-689-20586-4 **Atheneum**
0-689-71181-6 **Aladdin Paperbacks**
Newbery Medal
William Allen White Award
ALA Notable Children's Book

About the B'nai Bagels
0-689-20631-3 **Atheneum**

Altogether, One at a Time
0-689-20638-0 **Atheneum**
0-689-71290-1 **Aladdin Paperbacks**

A Proud Taste for Scarlet and Miniver
0-689-30111-1 **Atheneum**
ALA Notable Children's Book
National Book Award Nominee

The Second Mrs. Giaconda
0-689-70450-X **Aladdin Paperbacks**

Father's Arcane Daughter
* Coming spring 1999
0-689-82680-X **Aladdin Paperbacks**
YASD Best Book for Young Adults
IRA/CBC Children's Choice

Journey to an 800 Number
* Coming spring 1999
0-689-82679-6 **Aladdin Paperbacks**

Throwing Shadows
0-689-82120-4 **Aladdin Paperbacks**
ALA Notable Children's Book
American Book Award Nominee

Up From Jericho Tel
0-689-31194-X **Atheneum**
0-689-82120-4 **Aladdin Paperbacks**
ALA Notable Children's Book
Parents' Choice Award for Literature
NCTE Notable Children's Trade Book for the
Language Arts

Amy Elizabeth Explores Bloomingdale's
0-689-31766-2 **Atheneum**

T-backs, T-shirts, COAT, and Suit
0-689-31855-3 **Atheneum**

TalkTalk: A Children's Book Author
Speaks to Grown-ups
0-689-31993-2 **Atheneum**

The View from Saturday
0-689-80993-X **Atheneum**
0-689-81721-5 **Aladdin Paperbacks**
1997 Newbery Medal Winner
ALA Notable Children's Book

LOOK FOR THESE TITLES AT YOUR LOCAL LIBRARY ~~~

(George)

Samuel Todd's Book of Great Colors

Simon & Schuster Children's Publishing Division
where imaginations meet
1230 Avenue of the Americas New York, NY
10020
www.SimonSaysKids.com